Revenge

Poppy Stuart

Copyright © 2023 Poppy Stuart
All rights reserved.
Revised Edition
ISBN: 9798389840263

This book is in gratitude to Cornelia Funke, author of my favourite book, Inkheart. She has taught me so much and inspired me to write my own book.

For my mum and my twin brother, Finlay.

Revenge

Book 1

Revenge

My Sister's Fate

The old chair creaked under my weight as I was forcefully pushed down upon it. I shrugged off the rough hands that were gripping my collar and sat in stubborn silence. I shivered as goosebumps settled on my neck; it wasn't the cold that made me shiver but spreading dread that sat in the pit of my stomach. It was midnight, maybe later, and the hands that had seized me earlier were the hands of a criminal. Filthy blood-stained hands.

The door across from me opened and a small figure was pushed towards me, sending her tumbling to the wet floor. Scrambling to her feet she scarpered towards me shuddering at the nasty look that was being thrown her way. Letty Lane spat at the shadow at the door and cursed in German, her lips curving into an unpleasant sneer. I wanted to shuffle away from the girl standing next to me, for the look that had fallen over her face was murderous.

At the threshold of the room, however, the person only laughed, a ghastly rumble of a laugh. Letty pursed her lips, stepped forward and stuck out her tongue. The door was slammed in her face. Cussing once again, this time in Italian, she turned to me, her fire like hair matching her terrible temper. Letty, her cheeks red with her fury, opened her mouth and spat in English, "Well done you big oaf. Happy now, are we?"

The girl standing in front of me was my sister and she had quite a tongue; it could twist and form words of different languages; she spoke about 20 but she is still learning. I simply stared at her, not trusting myself to speak, earning an earful from her mirthless mouth. Shaking my head in denial, I slowly got to my feet and touched the wall to my right. It was cold like it was made from ice and the bars that let the sunshine into the damp room were so close together I could only manage to put my hand through it. Letty watched me with scathing eyes and once I had paced up and down for what seemed like the millionth time, she snapped, "Oh Roy! Stop kidding yourself, we're stuck and it's all your fault!" I looked at her and replied, "Well dearest Sister you're just a ball of sunshine today, aren't you?" She scoffed and rolling her eyes as she turned her back on me, crossed her arms. I was glad of that. That meant she wouldn't be saying anything to me for a while.

A couple of times I saw her tremble and a twinge of regret seeped into my mind. That was my fault, well, partly. I will not be so courteous as to take all the blame. Leonardo Marvella was the reason why we were there. I could tell you the story of how me and Letty got in that room, but I am sure that story will be clear soon enough.

As the sun fell beneath the mountains with white peaks, a chill fell over the room. No longer heated by the warmth of the sun, the room's temperature dropped dramatically. Out of the corner of my eye, I saw Letty shaking in the coldness, rocking back and forth on the heels of her feet and her teeth chattering together. Walking to her, I placed my arms around her neck and pulled her towards me. She huddled closer, thankful for the warmth my body provided. The only thing she and I were wearing were the clothes we had arrived in. In her case, a thin dress the colour of the amber tips of her tresses and a pair of white boots. I was wearing trousers and a t-shirt, and I wore no shoes.

I heard her muffled voice and looked down to see her tongue twisted in languages that were alien to me. She glowered up at me and if she was not my sister, I might have let go of her and let her freeze to death, but I didn't. The door creaked open, and an ugly face peered at us. It was wrinkly and heavily lined, a grey beard sat wispy under a chin and a pair of spectacles stared at us. He was so old he looked like a ghost, and his frail, twig like body hobbled towards us. A book sat under his elbow and his eyes twinkled not unfriendly at us.

"Master said to talk to you," He squeaked in an unnaturally high tone. Letty looked at me, a smile playing on her lips. She knew, like I did, that that old man was like Grandpa Eddie. Grandpa Eddie was our father's father, and he was as crippled and disabled as they could get but even with his differences, he was a kind soul. His skin below his eyes was so wrinkled that it made him squint. He spent his days in his armchair smoking a cigarette and reading the newspaper.

"Who are you?" I asked.

"John Parker."

He said no more but simply watched us over his spectacle's, his blue eyes twinkling. Catching each other's gaze my sister shrugged and mouthed just say some think nice.

"So, er."

"John, is fine laddie."

"Right, John what can we tell you?"

The man thought for so long I swear his wrinkles were growing wrinkles and finally, when he spoke, Letty was looking bored around the room, and I was rolling on the balls of my heels.

"Name?"

Letty nudged my foot and when I looked at her, she whispered, "Say something then, Duffus."

"Should I say our real names?"

"Course not idiot, make something up." Letty hissed at me and then she opened her gob and started swearing in French. She looked nervously from the old man to me twitching irritably.

"Tabitha and Leo Swash." I used the first names that came to my mind. For a split second, I thought he did not believe me but then he nodded. Taking the book from under his arm, grabbing a pen from his pocket, he began to scribble. Letty smiled in relief and took my hand threading her fingers through mine. I gave her a sideways look before saying to the old man, "Why are we here?"

He muttered to himself for a while, thinking if he was allowed to tell them and decided that he wasn't. He shook his head. Clinging to my arm, Letty watched John intently. "Tabitha, was it? Master, wants to speak to you." Letty just stared at him, the words she had just heard were hard for her to understand and I saw her bottom lip quiver as she spoke, "Ro- Leo is coming too." The old man shook his head. "No."

My sister looked on the verge of tears and when he beckoned for her to follow him, she clutched even harder to my arm. "Letty, just go," I whispered low enough that the old man could not hear. She turned her fearful eyes on me. My chest hardened; it pained me to see her in such despair. Letty let John guide her to the door but then stopped and took one final look at me; I nodded and waved. I was trying to be strong for her, but my mind just let its imagination play and I thought of the terrors that awaited her.

I closed my eyes and when I opened them again, she and the old man had vanished.

Looking to the past

Curse my brother! A good lot of nothing, that's what he is! No doubt he was safe in that cell back there and here I am being guided into a lion's den! Obviously, he was scared for me, practically shaking in his old rags that lay loose on his skinny body, but he was trying to cover that up by smiling. I hate when he does that. Roy can fool anyone in the world with just his charming smile and a confident whisper. Me. There is no way in this world he is fooling me - we have been inseparable since the womb.

The old man walked painfully slow, and I had the right mind to give him a good kick, but I have always had a soft spot for the elderly and something about the way he lifted himself up and walked made me think he didn't want to be here at all. He dragged his feet up the winding, stone, lantern lit corridors as he muttered to himself. Many cells stood on either side of me, bars the only thing keeping me a safe distant away from the potentially dangerous prisoners.

They all looked like there was no life left in them and if they had not sighed or groaned, I might have thought they were dead. Most of them were just skin and bones and thin cloth whilst a very few of them, perhaps new prisoners, were talking or else pacing up and down. I thought that if me and Roy stayed there as long as these men had, we might just turn into them. That place was a hell-house, it leeched your identity away, leaving you just an empty shell with everyone looking identical.

John stopped so abruptly that I knocked into him, and I had to reach out to catch him as he stumbled. "Sorry!" I apologised, setting him on his feet. He stood still, his mouth ajar and a rather peculiar expression taking hold of his lined face. Not knowing what to do, I put my hands up as if that would do anything and whispered, "Are you alright?" Again, he just stared, an incredulous look spreading across his lined, wise, old profile.

It was only when the door opened that he moved, and even then, his eyes did not leave mine. He was looking at me so intensely that I did not realise the hands reaching for me from the door. A spew of curses left my mouth, and I yelped as I was pulled into the room. Before I could see the person, who had set his hands on me, he turned so I could only see his back. The only thing I knew for sure was that he was a man, as no woman in this world had such broad shoulders, short hair, or no curves.

"Who are you?" I asked. He just stood there like he was a statue. "I said who are you?" The bitterness of my tongue was forming words I knew would be unwise to say to this man. He still did not answer me. Anger boiled inside of me, and I swore to God if he did not answer me, if he carried on standing there, I might have killed him. How? I had not a clue but at that moment I felt I could have killed him with my bare hands.

"98. Report." 98? What kind of name is that? To my pure amazement John Parker answered him.

"Girl is Tabitha Swash; brother is in the other room. Leo is his name." John wheezed these words and closed his eyes like all of his energy had been drained from him. I watched him nervously as he swayed slightly. "Is that what they told you?" the man laughed. Shuffling backwards, I glanced to the door wanting to dart behind it and run back to Roy. Circling his desk, he turned his chair so we would not be able to see him and sat down.

"Tabitha come here." I obliged. I stood next to the chair but did not look at him. A wave of nausea fell over me as a fetid smell of cigarettes and beer greeted my nose.

"Do you know why you are here Tabitha?" Maybe it was the way he said the name Roy had come up with that made my insides melt into each other. I tried not to stutter but the words came out almost inaudibly. I felt his eyes on me, but I did not look back at him. Closing my eyes, I spoke again but not in English. I find English the hardest language to speak when the world is spinning away, and hope seems but a slither. German came out fast and furious. I told him no I didn't. I did not expect him to understand but I had to say something.

But perhaps he had understood what I had said because he responded, "Your here because I need you to do something for me."

I stayed silent. It will always be the same, I figure. The world. Powerful men will aways be greedy, unsatisfied. Roy has aways had a different view on the world. He has always told me, Letty, there are only two types of people in this world. There are the moths in the story, they are always drawn to the flames. When you are the flames, well, you make the moths drawn to you.

I suppose that I was the 'moth' but later, thinking back to that day, I could argue that I was the 'flame'. He was drawn to me; he was the one who wanted my presence, who summoned me. Standing in that eerie silence, I realised how strange it was that my life had turned to this. I felt like my insides were on fire and at that very moment I would have loved nothing more than to sink into the floorboards.

I blamed Roy entirely for this, of course. Pig-headed idiot. Throwing cash left right and centre and not even checking who he has made the deal with. Bargaining with the likes of Leonardo Marvella. The son of the Devil himself. Spends his days as the living Satan, ruining lives and ending them. Two particular people in mine and Roy's life were murdered by his hands.

A story for another time, I think.

The man cleared his throat and ordered. "Your real name, you two faced Pithan." The cheek of that man was unbelievable. I opened my mouth and the words that had sat on the tip of my tongue fell out. John gasped in utter shock and amazement, as I cursed more wildly than a drunk person. I knew there was no escape the trap of the lie my brother had weaved and I spoke not to the man but the window, staring at it intently, "Can you imagine? He thinks, because he is big man, he can make me talk." If somebody had been sitting outside the window peering in, they might have thought I was mad. Just like Grandpa Eddie.

I heard the chair being scraped away and the ringing of my ears, as my cheek burned. The force of the slap sent me tumbling to the floor. "Oh, Gracious me!" John Parker squeaked, covering his eyes. I lay there a crumpled heap of clothes and flesh.

The greying world

I should have been next to Letty, protecting her, shielding her from the world around us. But there I was sitting on the floor, a nobody. I felt stripped of my title, Roy Lane, a well-known family disgraced with his worthless name. It pained me to think my sister stayed with me, when she could have been at the boarding school for ladies. In fact, it practically made me sick to my stomach to think of such things.

By that time, my stomach let out a low rumble, and I realised I had not eaten for 24 hours. The last time I had eaten was at Grandpa Eddie's the day before. Getting up, I walked to the door and bending down looked through the keyhole. I saw a hall stretched wide, it looked like everything was bleached in a dull grey - the walls, the floor, the bars on the windows. Even the people seemed grey in their own way.

I pulled back and gazed around my cell. It was slightly wider than the hall but not by much and apart from its higher ceiling, it was identical. Crouching down, I looked through the hole to find someone staring dead into my eyes. I shivered and jumped back, one hand on my heart to feel its wild beat. A cackle came from outside and the door clunked and swung open. "Out! Now!" The guard shouted and grabbing me by the collar, he dragged me away.

The faces that stared at me were skulls with their skin pulled tight around it. I gulped and carried on walking; they reached out to me from their cells. "Help me!" they whispered. "Curse you, Roy Lane!" Others that knew me shrieked, rattling the bars. I stared at the floor, ashen faced. The guard pulled me to a door, I protested but he pushed me inside. My body collided with the cold stone floor, and I felt bruises forming all over as I ached.

Small, the room had a resemblance to a cage you might see in the zoo. Somewhere for the animal to sleep – a straw mattress. A place where the creature can do his business - a bucket. Somewhere where they can get food - a rectangular hole in the wall next to the door for food to be passed inside.

It was simply a dull cell.

It was only then I realised what a privilege it was to have had a safe roof over my head, to have been able to leave and go whenever I pleased and to have the decision on what I wanted to eat. But then I turned into a traitor in the opposing sides domain. A fish without its water.

The door creaked open, and light flooded the dim room. A child like shadow stood in the doorway. The figure was pushed forward, and the door swung shut.

I was quiet for a while as I thought on what to say or if to say anything at all. A girl's voice spoke first and that made a sigh leave my lips. "Roy?" It was soft hush of a whisper and when I let out a cry the figure hurried towards me. Letty threw her arms around me and burrowed her head in my neck.

The price we pay for money

The familiar smell of orange greeted my nose, and I closed my eyes to bathe in its comfort. The soft fabric of my brother's t-shirt stroked my cheek, making me huddle closer to him. Small voices lingered with arrogant one's outside. There was shouting and laughter, shrieking and pleading, and then a silence crept into the air. The blackness of my eyelids made me try to imagine me and Roy, somewhere else, maybe sitting by the fire listening to Grandpa Eddie turning the pages of his newspaper. I tasted the words I had been ordered to tell Roy. Poison on my tongue.

I looked up at his brilliantly blue eyes with tears crusading down my face. I told him, "We have to give him 4 million pounds." He just stared at me, disbelief edged on his face. I felt something wet splash onto my hair as I held him tight. "We can get it Roy." I whispered softly. "We can get it."

Only God knows how we were going to get that money. But we had to otherwise our life was going to be cut extremely short.

The next day had come indolently slow. When I awoke and sat up on the straw mattress, I saw Roy huddled in the other corner of the room and I knew he had not slept. Dark circles under his eyes gave him away and I saw the way his head drooped. He looked around helplessly. It was a cold morning and the sun offered us no warmth as its beams of light filled the room.

We sat in timid silence, and it seemed the only thing we had too much of. Time. It ticked by painfully as we awaited our release from the cell. Though I had slept, I felt as drained and weary as if I had not. Maybe because my nightmares awoke me often that night. The man, the face I had never seen haunted me and I found myself awfully curious to what he looked like.

The clunk of boots in the hall made me stand and face the door but Roy stayed where he was. A guard stood in the doorway, and he stepped aside so we could leave. I grabbed Roy's hand and pulled him to his feet guiding him to the door and out into the corridor. The prisoners looked longing at us as we passed them and I saw the way they glared at Roy in suppressant fury. They looked at me pleadingly, beggingly. I couldn't help them, so, I walked away, not giving any of them a second glance. I still regret it now. The guard led us into a stone courtyard.

I cried out.

Corpses sat with no dignity on the floor, wasting away. The wind blew a ghostly breath and death lingered in the air like a monument, a terrible reminder. A naked little boy lay in the middle of the floor, blood poured from his blue, cold lips, and he shook with his sobs of pain.

I wanted to reach down and hold him in my arms, to rock him and to tell him everything was alright so he might not die alone. His hair was as white as snow, with frost like blue tips, and he looked at me and I began to cry. He looked so horribly confused. His eyes told me he was scared, that he wanted to go home. He was too young to understand, to know that his death would shake the core of the Earth. Even I didn't know at that time who that boy was but when I found out I promise you this.

I will revenge him!

When Roy saw him, I thought he would burst into tears too, but he glanced away, staring at his own feet. The guard that had stood next to us, pushed us forward and barked. "Move!" We walked to the edge of the courtyard, and he opened the gate. It was an iron gate, twice the size of me, towering high into the air. Intimidating for any potential escapers. I gently nudged Roy forward, so he stepped out of the courtyard and into a field in front of us. When I went to follow, I was yanked back as the guard took a handful of my hair. He breathed in my face, "Remember scum. Remember your mission. Come without it and you die."

I tried to pull away, but he held me fast, "You'll need them." I stopped struggling and peered over the man's shoulder, there two black horses stood behind him. The guard let go, shoving me slightly backwards. I walked to the magnificent creatures and stroked one of their heads in my hands. It felt rough but not unpleasant and going to the horse's side I lifted myself into its saddle. Roy was already sitting astride the other horse and he dug his heels into its side to make it start in a trot.

He was distant to me, as we rode and Roy made sure his horse was always ahead of me. When I had had enough of the dreary silence, I called to him, "You know sulking isn't going to change anything? So just come here and let's make a plan." He just ignored me and trotted faster into the start of a canter. I followed. "Roy!" I yelled. "Roy, I didn't come with you for nothing. Let me help you!"

"Just go Letty." The coldness in his voice made my voice change from pleading to furious.

"Ungrateful Pig! Leave? Leave!" I shrieked.

"We are never going to get our hands on that amount of money Letty. I don't want you here when he kills me. He will kill you too." I hear his steady words, watch as they drift to me but instead of making me sympathetic, they made me want to show him my wrath.

"You fool!" I screamed and I caught up to him striding side by side. I glared into his face and saw a boy. A boy who was scared, frightened. "I don't need you to protect me. I never have. Oh, don't you see I am not a little girl anymore. I want to do this. With you. We will get our hands on that money Roy. We will."

He looked at me. My brother stared at me with a hysterical expression building on his face. The horse he was riding slowed into a walk and Roy, shifting a wary glance behind his shoulder at the grey building behind us, whispered, "Alright."

The horse's gallop was slowed down by snow that fell thick and fast. Crystals of falling ice bestowed the grass with its light weight as it settled on everything it could touch, bleaching the world in a white cloak. Our only source of time was the sun, the glorious star in the sky that hung above us as a clock and yet a compass.

My stomach growled and I felt its emptiness, felt its groans for food. A yearning I could not fulfil. No human or otherwise passed us, and I could not see any puffs of smoke riding high in the air. We were alone, completely, and utterly alone.

The snow had been replaced by droplets of water. I looked up at the sky and stuck out my tongue feeling the soft splatter of the raindrops. My parched throat felt desperately numb as I watched as the water fell. Roy was out of his saddle, leaning on the back of his horse's neck and lying on the black magnificent creatures back.

"Roy!" I chided him, "Roy, that's dangerous! You could fall and then I would have to drag your butt back on that horse and pray to God you're not hurt!"

"Chill Letty, you act as though I would die!"

I glowered at him then turning away muttered darkly under my breath, "If it does not kill you, I will."

"What was that?"

"Nothing," I spat, rolling my eyes, "Not that it was any of your business."

He scoffed at that and swung himself back into the saddle. I dug my heel into my horse's sides and called to her, "Go!"

New friends

We stopped at a town hours later and gave the horses to a stable boy to look after. Letty and I began to walk around the town. Sellers called out to us, "A necklace for the lady?" "Perfume! Perfume! Come and get your perfume!" "What a pretty girl! A flower for your friend?"

The streets were cobbled but winding and little kids ran wild, rushing through crowds of buyers and slipping pieces of unpaid bread or fruit in their pockets. Rich with the fragrance of spices and perfume the air wafted into our noses making them tingle. We observed from our place in the crowd, a man selling bread and we fought our way through the plethora of people to get to him. "Two rolls please." I asked. The man looked at us for a while, staring at us up and down. Then he nodded, grabbed two rolls, put them in a cloth then handed it to us. He put his hand out and said, "That'll be two pounds."

"I'm sorry. We do not have any money?" I blinked at him. He snarled at us then snatched the bread out of my hands and spat on my face. Letty cried out and started swearing at the man in a language I could not quite figure out. The man did not understand the fast, furious tongue being whipped at him, but he knew what she was probably shouting at him. He waved to two people in green camouflage suits and snarled at us, "Don't be so crude with me little girl! To have a knife for a tongue won't go down well here!"

One of the men holding a gun waddled towards us picking something beige from his teeth, one hand on his vast belly. He grunted, "'Ello 'Ello 'Ello what seems to be the problem here then Sir?"

"These two, officer, grovelling me for bread! Free bread! Imagine that! The cheek of youth these days. Would you ever get spoken too in such manner in my days? No, Sir, you would not!" The man who had been selling bread's, chin jutted as he spoke. Letty's cheeks burned hot red, and she opened her mouth, her eyes raging balls of fury, "We did no such thing! Grovelling! We don't want your mouldy bread anyway!" I put a hand in warning on her arm as the man's eyes bulged. The officer watched the scene lazily scratching his behind, and his expression was one of a camel. His bottom lip stuck out and his eyes remained half closed.

Letty shrugged off my arm and snarled at the man dangerously. "Now, now, now miss. That is no way to act to your elders!" The green dressed officer patronised. My sister, turned very slowly to the officer and stared at him, eyes wild, looking at him dead in the eye. He put a hand on his gun and slowly pulled it out, pointing it directly at Letty. She did not bat an eyelid. "Stupid, stupid girl!"

Not thinking, she lunged. I caught her around the waist as she threw herself at the officer, thrashing and yelling in my arms. "Letty! Letty what is the matter with you?"

She shrieked and shouted, "How dare you! I'm starving and you cannot even saver two rolls? Maybe instead of eating for three, you could eat for one and give me and my brother the rest!" The officer might have a gun, a weapon, but my sister needed no dangerous thing to hold, to threaten, she had her mouth as deadly and as sharp as any dagger or gun for that.

Wordlessly, I dragged her away as she fought against my hold. Stunned, the two men just watched and so did shoppers nearby. I hauled her to an alleyway where no one walked by and sat her on the floor. She glowered up at me. I crouched down to peer into her face and asked, "Letty we have only been here for minutes, and you have already lit a fuse. You do amaze me at the best of times."

"Excuse me?" A timid voice came from nearby and I looked up to see a lady. She wore a dress that scraped the floor and a corset that hugged her body. Her hair was in curls and in a clip to stop it falling in her face and she wore two white gloves on her hands. A basket hung in the crook of her arm, and she beamed at us, "I am sorry I could not help but to overhear your, um, conversation with the men."

"So what?" Letty growled. I flicked her on the nose and shushed her.

"Can we help you?"

"Yes. I am a writer, author, actress and you are the fire, anger, fury that I need," She swished a hand to Letty and then looked at me, eyes twinkling, "And you, the gentlemen, peacekeeper, hero of the story. I got the rolls for you too." She patted the basket and smiled at us.

She told us to follow her and so she led us to a wide road that seemed the only road people did not wander in. It wound its way out of the town into a hill. On top of that green mound was a mansion. A magnificent fountain, with statues of cupid surrounding it, stood as a roundabout in the centre of a circle shaped road. The mansion was a block of white stone with pillars keeping it upright and many windows in neat rows up and down.

The lady began to walk up the cobbled, human free road and I must admit I was stunned how she could walk in such a straight line with such small heels. Letty was the first to follow the lady and I followed shortly after. Me and my sister had to hold onto each other's arm to not fall, and our ankles were sore with the plethora of ways they had twisted. She, the lady, rapped on the door and it was opened seconds later by a man in a black and white suit. The lady threw the basket in the man's arms and smiled at her home.

It was even more wonderful inside than it was outside. The floor was so clean it was like a mirror and gold settled with the white walls and ceilings now. A vast staircase that was the width of the spacious room sat at the back of the grand area. There was a golden banister curled at the top and end of the staircase, but it was flat in the middle so someone's hand could easily glide upon it.

Letty's eyes seemed to be growing wider and wider the more she looked around.

"It is beautiful, isn't it my darlings?" I jumped. I had forgotten about the lady as I had been too absorbed in the wonderful room. Letty nodded silently and I saw out of the corner of my eye Letty pinching herself to check this was no dream. A smile grazed my lips as I took my sister's elbow and guided her up the stairs. She placed her hand on the banister and I knew she was thinking of home. Home was never this grand, but we did have a sweeping staircase with a banister just like this one.

The lady stopped outside a beautiful purple door and said, "Oh my! Where are my manners?" She turned to us and smiling told us, "I am Lady Evelyn. You may call me Roxanne though." Lady

Evelyn or Roxanne as we told to call her reached out to take Letty's hand, "What is your name, my love?"

"Letty. Letty Lane." My sister answered her.

Roxanne's brows furrowed, "Letty? Is that you real name?"

"It's Violette but everyone calls me Letty." My sister answered as she shifted uncomfortably. Roxanne looked at Letty and she seemed to be thinking and then she smiled sweetly and decided, "Letty it is then. Though it is always proper to use the actual name for things." She did not ask me what my name was but simply opened the purple door and said, "Your room will be this one, I think. Stay as long as you need. You must have travelled far. Samantha shall sort you out, I must be off now my darlings." She clapped her hands and a maid popped out of nowhere. Waving, she hurried away, her heels clacking as she went.

The maid waited patiently as me and Letty made our way into the room. "Oh wow," Letty cried, she spun around the room her arms outstretched. She ran to the plump, over the top with decoration, bed and jumped on it. I laughed; she was like a little kid. A hearth with a fire crackling inside sat by the other side of a door. Samantha walked to the door which sat opposite to the bed and opened it. She stood next to it waiting for me and Letty to go in first. I went over to Letty and took her hand as she hopped down and ran to the next room.

I heard a squeal and then a gasp and when I went in, I knew why. A room even bigger than the bedroom stood before us, racks and racks of dresses and smart suits lined the walls. Samantha smiled at Letty and asked, "Would you like to try one on Miss?" Being called 'Miss' seemed too much for Letty as she was stumped into silence. Taking her quietness as a, 'Yes', the maid held a light blue dress and handed it to my sister.

When she came out of the closet in the dress, even I had to admit she looked the definition of beautiful. It was off the shoulder and the sleeves were thin material and sat loose on her upper arm. A sky-blue corset hugged her body from her waist to the top her breasts, it was decorated with white flowers at the top and bottom. The bottom of her dress flowed and was poofy and layered. It showed her feet that wore tiny blue heels and a trail billowed behind her. Her hair was curled, and the top half was placed into a blue ribbon, the dress drew out her sapphire piercing blue eyes that were round globes on her tanned face.

A decision of change

I felt like a princess out of a fairy-tale and I looked like one too. The dress felt light on my body, and I felt as though I was about to attend a ball. My brother seemed to blush as I walked out of the closet and Samantha looked thoroughly pleased with herself. Roxanne had money alright, money we desperately needed.

The man had not said how much time we had but he didn't really strike me as a guy who had patience. Me and Roy sat on the bed munching on the rolls, my throat was dry, and they tasted ever so slightly stale. The room smelt of lavender, fresh and clean. I heard the echoes of talking from downstairs and occasionally the clunk of heels. The sheets felt soft under my fingers, but the bed sunk when someone sat on it, and it reminded me a lot of a marshmallow. I saw Roy out of the corner of my eye, and he seemed lost in his own thoughts.

It hurt me to think that there was a wall between us, and I wanted to break it down. "Roy." I spoke. "Roy, I don't blame you anymore for losing all our money and bargaining with that monster." He looked at me and I thought I saw a tear in his eyes and a wobble of a smile but then he turned back to his stale bread and simply answered, "Thank you. That means a lot." I laughed and threw myself on him. Normally he would have pushed me off but that time he let me hug him and I smelt in his aroma of orange.

"Letty."

"Roy?" I looked up at him from my place in his arms.

"Letty, wouldn't you feel guilty from stealing from Roxanne? She has been good to us."

"Roy." I said sternly, "Roy if there was another way, I promise you we would take it but there is none. This our chance to survive and it looks like she could risk losing 4 million pounds."

It was a horrible thing to say, I know. But I had to convince myself and my brother somehow. We were silent for so long after I said those words and I knew in my gut's things were going to turn even more terrible. There was another chamber next to the one me and Roy had sat eating but for some reason I could not bear to be even five steps away from my brother. I slept in a dreamless sleep that night and morning came with dread and guilt.

Roxanne had set off into town early the next morning, so, to mine and Roy's relief, we did not have to face her. I wore the sky-blue dress that day and oh, how I felt like royalty. Even Roy wore a handsome suit. It was an olive-green suit jacket with a white under coat and matching olive-green trousers. Samantha greeted us when we went downstairs into the grand room in the front of the house and she gave us 300 pounds each and said, "Miss, Sir, Lady Evelyn has given me this for you to spend in town. I will attend to you today. Would you like to leave now or breakfast first?"

"I think breakfast first Samantha," I answered glancing at Roy. He nodded back at me and together we followed Samantha to a dining hall. It was a purple room. A dusk purple wallpaper decorated the walls and the grand chairs that sat around the long table had plump light purple cushions on them. Two men in black and white suits pulled out two chairs for me and Roy and when we sat across to each other they tucked us in. Maids came from the opposite door from which we had come in and put out a plate of eggs, bacon, and all sorts of rare fruit in front of both me and Roy.

My mouth watered as I ate the food. "Oh. It is delicious!" I cried looking up at the maids. They looked at me with shock on their faces for a few seconds and then giving each other a disbelieving look beamed back at me. We set off after the sumptuous food had been devoured and headed into town. Samantha called us a carriage with two white horses pulling it. The carriage was a warm, yellow and was open with a sunroof on top. We settled onto it and Samantha whispered to the coachman and off we went. It was a remarkably smooth ride, and my ankles thanked me for not walking down that treacherous hill.

The mirthless heat of the raging ball of fire that hung in the sky made my cheeks grow so hot that I had to try to fan myself with my hands. Roy took off his suit jacket and undid a few of the top buttons of his under coat but I could do nothing but sweat. When we reached a road that people walked on, they cleared a path for us, and I saw children pointing at us and tugging on their mother's sleeve. One little girl that stood near the carriage whispered to her mother, "Mummy look at the lady, she is beautiful!" I smiled at this.

The carriage rolled to a stop in front of a shop. The shop was bleached in the sun to a creamy yellow and a man in a bright lemon colour suit pranced out of the building and held his hand out to me and exclaimed in French, "Pretty Lady, what a pretty Lady!"

I thanked him as I curtseyed. He stared at me, he said to me in English in a deep French accent, "You know French

Mademoiselle?"

"Yes, I know many languages." I answered him.

He looked impressed and smiling, said to me, "I like you; you must come into my shop." And so, me and Roy did go into his shop and how strange it was. There were two of everything, there were tea sets and clothes, rugs, and utensils. Anything you could possibly need was here. Everything was so random that I could not help to smile. It was the craziest, most wonderful shop I had ever been in. It was the most haphazardly way to organize his things by hanging them off the ceiling and have shelves wonky and placed randomly across the floor.

"What a beautiful sun umbrella," I reached to stroke the wood of the handle and turned it in my hands. It had little robins and bluetits and flowers decorating it and it smelt a lot of fields. The wet damp smell of the grass and the aroma of the fresh air. "How much?" I asked in French. He told me a price and I turned to Samantha, "If you would Samantha."

Looking around the shop I bought a fan, a delightful orange and counted the coins in my hands.

With the day stretched out in front of us, me and Roy left, waving to the man, and exiting the shop. We talked in hushed, urgent tones whenever we were alone to say what was to be done about the money. The biggest problem of all is we had not a clue where the money was but surely people like Roxanne would not keep it lying around.

"Well, she must have to go to it at some point," Roy whispered as we sat huddled in a corner of a street. Lifting my fan so it covered my mouth I hissed back, "And when will that be? We do not have long I suspect. The hourglass continuously runs, and we stand here and do nothing."

I smelt roses and something sweet and I looked around me, flowers had bloomed on vines that crept on the walls around us. The air had become a stuffy wave of humidity and the warmth of the sun was starting to take its toll on the people. They muttered under their breath as they dragged their feet; they hurried to a patch of shade or else walked into a cool shop. As the afternoon ticked by painfully slow, me and Roy made our way back to the mansion.

Wrath and retribution

Letty's temper shone as brightly as the blazing ball of fire in the sky. She walked through the crowd, a moody expression taking hold of her features. Samantha called us a carriage to take us up to the pristine white building on top of the hill. When we climbed in, my sister swore at the driver, shouting at him to hurry up in German. "Letty!" I chided, "Letty don't be so rude!" I wish I hadn't spoken, for her wicked tongue turned on me and she shouted at me, her cheeks turning pink with her fury. I was ever so glad at that moment that I did not know the language of which she spoke.

Samantha looked hastily at her feet when the glowering eyes of my sister turned on her. I watched as Letty's chest rose and fell and she looked as if she was going to throttle someone. However, I reached for her hand and squeezed. She turned her blue eyes on me, and I smiled as the hard glare washed away to a soft smile.

Letty, holding fast to my hand, glanced at the town around us. It was the town that played the part of our asylum in our story, the place where we sought shelter, safety and was given it on a golden platter. Trust was a fool's game and believe me when I tell you I wanted nothing less than to betray Roxanne.

We rolled up to the mansion and I hopped down, lending Letty a hand. Hitching up her dress, Letty climbed the stairs leading to the grand doors and rapped on the wooden planks. It was swung open, and we all entered. Letty froze and I heard her splutter, "Hello." I gazed at the person Letty was talking to and had to swallow a gasp.

Roxanne stood in front of us in a clean, sweeping gown of lemon coloured silk. Smiling charmingly at me and my sister, she told us, "I was thinking darlings and I came up with the most marvellous idea," her eyes traced up and down our outfits and her smile seemed to falter but then she beamed and carried on, "How about a Ball, a grand one at that, every Lady and Lord in the land should be invited. That is an excellent way to introduce you to everyone. Of course, then it will all be, write, write, write, and act, act, act."

She waved and swished her hands in the air as she spoke and looking at us asked, "Now my darlings, is there anyone you should like to invite? Maybe some friends? Hmm? No? Well then, I guess the guest list is all up to me." Clapping her hands in excitement, she let out a little squeal of delight before snapping her fingers at the butler and left the room, the man following her.

"My God! Is she ever not happy?" My sister groaned.

When we got to our bedroom, she ran to the bed and buried her face in the pillow. "You know Letty, it wouldn't hurt for us to enjoy ourselves. Or is it you have forgotten how to have fun?" At that she picked up the pillow and threw it at me. I laughed and caught it. Grabbing hold of the pillow I swung around and let go, I did not see it hit her but when I looked at Letty, she was lying on the bed on her back with the soft rectangular marshmallow on her face.

Sitting up, she laughed, "Cheeky!" and threw it back at me but that time I did not see it coming and was slapped in the face. I picked up the pillow from its solemn place on the floor at my feet and walked to the bed, settling it back where it was supposed to be. "What is the point of a Ball, Roy? It is just more time wasted with the meaningless pleasure of your supposed fun." Letty said to me sitting up, her brows furrowed together. For that, I had no answer but, on that night, I wanted to dance my fears and troubles away, I wanted to be so drunk, that I passed out.

She knew what I yearned for, what I desired to keep my sanity. It always confused me how she knew. Sometimes it was almost as if she knew me better than I knew I myself. The day had drained me, but it was late, perhaps past midnight when I actually drifted to a dreamless sleep...

I sensed movement in the room and the unnerving feeling I was being watched. Breathing came from my side of the bed and I was scared an eyelid might flutter or twitch. Something soft was pressed against my cheek and I smelled in the aroma of flowers. Lying across one side of my body somebody nuzzled closer into my neck. Whispering floated to me and I felt a shadow fall across my face. I wanted to scream and run but I willed myself to remain still, to not give myself away.

Another thing grazed my cheek as it pulled back the soft something and stroked it. The person in my arms let out a sigh then slept peacefully on. As quickly as it had come, the owners of the whispering had gone and the room was left empty of intruders. I opened my eyes and looked down. Silk, amber tresses sat sprawled on my shoulder and you could see where the shadow like figure had stroked the hair away from the face.

Pushing Letty off me, I stepped out of the bed and stood. My sister shivered as a draft sneaked its way under the covers. Smiling, I leaned over and tucked her in more, watching the way her hair lay around her face and around her. She stopped quivering and I left the room. The hallways looked creepy in the dark, as shadows that I thought belonged to humans lurked in the corners.

With every flicker of a candle, or a rustle of a curtain I jumped. The back of my neck was covered in goosebumps and my hands clammy and sweat covered. Creaking of floorboards made me stop in my tracks. I was at the top of the grand stairs now.

A whisper. A soft laugh. I breathed. I looked up. And...

There! A figure standing on the stairs, the shadow-like figure moving as it walked downwards. I shouted. It shot a glare up at me and looked directly in my eyes. A chill fell over me, but I ignored it and called for help running towards the nearest hall, then I turned back.

It was gone....

"Are you sure dear?" Roxanne asked coaxingly, "Somebody in my house?"

"Yes Roxanne. I am sure." I confirmed. Letty stood arms crossed leaning against the door as she watched us with beady eyes. The flame of the candle she held flickered as a breath of the wind flew over to her from the open window. "No, no. I am sorry darling but no. No! You must have just imagined it," Roxanne looked at me scathingly then clapped her hands and ordered, "Out! Out! Go and get some sleep. You're obviously so dreary-you are delusional. No. I am sorry, Mr Lane but get out. Its past midnight for Christ's sake!"

Roxanne's chambers that smelt heavily of perfume was piled high with books and pieces of paper. Her bed seemed the only thing clutter free. I felt a hand on my arm and gazed at the sleepy face of Letty. She smiled sleepily at me and murmured, "C'mon. Let's get to bed. Its freezing in here."

I obliged. As Letty dragged her feet towards our room, she told me, "I believe you, you know. You would never lie about something like this." Linking arms with her, I answered, "Thank you. I knew you would."

The coldness of the air made me shiver and I felt eyes on my back. The unnerving feeling that I was being watched kept me glancing over my shoulder. When we got to our room, I stopped Letty and told her, "I'll be back. Just going to get some water."

In the firelight, I saw her eyes twinkle with concern and her brows to furrow together, "Should I come too?" I shook my head and smiled wryly.

"Alright, let me get you a candle! Last thing we need is you falling down the stairs."

Walking over to an unlit candle, she lit it with the one in her hand and carried both of them to me. "Here." She passed it over. Before I could leave, she reached out to touch my cheek and leaned in to whisper into my ear, "You better not be doing anything stupid." She called me something in German then smiled, kissed my cheek, and retired to our room.

I made my way down the stairs, passed the place the figure had been. Creaking the door open, I swerved around the tall table on which we had eaten breakfast the previous morning and entered the kitchen. It was a wide stretch of white stone. It was warm as if a fire had just been burning and smelt heavily of spice and rich food.

Setting the candle on a worktop, I took a glass from its place in its cupboard and filled it with water. I sipped at it, feeling the coolness drip down my throat. Someone coughed in the room, and I slowly turned to see a black figure standing next to my candle. He leaned over, took a breath, and blew it out. I was forced into a blackness, and I felt the glass slip from my grip to shatter on the floor. The water spilled over my bare feet as I heard a whisper calling to me. "Leo. Leo. Leo."

"Who are you? Where are you?"

"Oh, but you know. You know! You know!" he repeated those two words over and over again until they turned into a cackle of mad laughter. I looked around helplessly until I felt a hand on my shoulder. I froze. I felt the scream leave my lips. "Letty!!!!!!" Again, hoots of laughter and then a chorus of, "You know! You know!" followed.

Everything stopped. The laughter ceased and the weight of the hand on my shoulder was gone. I turned around to see Letty standing there, glass in hand. "He ran for it! The coward ran! There! Out the door!" She pointed to the open door at the back of the kitchen. A spew of curses followed, and she held up her middle finger to the door. I grabbed her hand and pushed it down.

"Letty!" I cried as I saw blood smeared on the glass.

Grimacing she answered, "It is not mine."

Roxanne hurried into the room, "Now what on Earth is...." she stopped her eyes staring at the scene. "Are you alright?"

"Yes." Letty snarled, eyes flashing, "Maybe next time when someone tells you a person broke into your house you might take heed!"

"And that is why you are my flame darling Letty!"

Rolling her eyes, my sister grabbed my hand and dragged me upstairs leaving Roxanne alone in the kitchen. We sat on the bed.

"He called you Leo Swash?" Letty's voice was coated in worry as she eyed me with unease.

"Yes."

"Oh Roy, it was him. The man's whose face I never saw." My sister cried as her hand shot up to cover her mouth.

"How does he know where we are?"

"I don't know." Letty whimpered, "Roy! What do we do?"

"We get our hands on that money!"

Dresses and suits

The Ball was coming up fast and before I knew it, it was happening that night. That morning, Roxanne's servants and maids hurried about in a flurry of cloth and paper and Samantha was the only maid I was able to talk to as she dashed by. "Samantha?"

She stopped mid-run and smiled, "Good morning Miss! Do you need help getting ready?" I nodded and she called to another maid and gave her lists of jobs that needed to be done before she turned to me and apologized, "Beg pardon Miss but I shall just be a jiffy. If you would wait for me in your chambers."

When I got to the room, I saw Roy sitting at the end of the bed. He was staring at the floor, deep in thought. "Roy? What's wrong?" I asked standing in the doorway. Glancing at me, he put on one of his dashing fake smiles and answered, "It is nothing! Nothing!"

"No. It is not 'nothing', but I shall let it slide. Now, go and mope somewhere else Samantha is coming to help me."

"Yes, Your Majesty!" he mock-bowed as he sidled away.

"Miss?" Samantha stepped into the room. Two maids carrying a tub walked in and placed it on the floor by the hearth. A servant came in and filled it with steaming water from a bucket. After some trips downstairs, it was filled. Helping me undress, Samantha chatted excitedly away, "Now Miss, all of the dresses you have are lovely but none of them quite have the look that a Ball requires. Mistress did not pay me well the last couple of months and I could not ask you to use your money on such petty things, so I made you one. With the help of Betty and Maria of course." The two maids nodded in agreement.

I just stared at them as Betty scrubbed my hair enthusiastically and Maria left to go and get a towel. "Your hair is lovely Miss, like flowing threads of the sunlight," Betty complimented, dunking my head under the water. When I resurfaced, Maria stood arms poised in front of her with a white towel laid on top of her hands. Samantha took it and wrapped it around me before settling me on a chair by the fire to dry and sending the two maids to go and get the dress.

"You needn't have made me a dress; it must have taken you ages." I told her.

"Nonsense! Now, hush!"

The door creaked open, and I almost fell out of my chair. The most beautiful dress stood before me. It was a gown fit for a Queen. Its colour was the black sky that winked down at us, golden swirls lay the colour of stars at the hem of the magnificent skirt that sat around me. The dip in-between my breasts was decorated with more of the swirling gold and my shoulders and forearms were left bare as there was no sleeve. Samantha turned me so my back was facing her, and she tightened the corset. It moulded against my breast and showed off my curves splendidly not pinching or binding.

My hair now dried had been sectioned and put up. Half of the locks had been twisted into a crown braid, with golden and black beads on top, whilst the rest were curled and left to do as they pleased as they tumbled down on my back. Tiny heels were slid onto my feet, they were black and dull, but it did not matter- no one could see them anyway.

The door opened, and Roy strutted in. "Woah! Sorry Your Majesty wrong room! I was looking for my ugly sister."

"Haw, haw, haw. Very funny." I laughed. He held out the crook of his arm to me and re-arranging my skirts I walked to the door. With both of the doors open, I could just manage to glide through. My heart tripled its pace and I felt behind my makeup sweat forming. Thousands of faces looked up at me and I heard gasps and cries from the crowd bellow. Elegantly, I hovered down the stairs keeping my eyes on the people.

From the sea of gowns and suits, a rather flustered Roxanne made her way towards us. "Where did you get the gown? Violette?" She looked over it scathingly and then down at her own ballgown – it looked as dull as dishwater next to a beautiful swan.

"Is there a problem with it?" I asked, eyes narrowing.

Gritting her teeth, she put a hand through her hair and answered, "Of course not."

"Great." I muttered, then when Roxanne's back was towards me, I leaned towards Roy and called her a lot of rude names in Italian. Roy had not a clue what I had said but he got the gist and held back a smile.

"My friends, "Roxanne cooed in a delighted tone, "We are here tonight to rejoice in my new stars. Lady and Lord Lane." There was cheer, followed by clapping. The silence droned on, as Roxanne began to speak again, "We are here for friendship, trust and money!"

Money? Now it was my turn to give her a scathing look. Money? That is why we're here tonight for money? The only thing that it is, is the heart of evil, the witch of the story. Enchanted to look like a dream, a chance at peace and power to attract foolish men and women and then reveal itself for its deception and power to control with greed.

Then there was more clapping then, as one, everyone began to move. Already people were swirling each other around and I saw the way they looked into each other's eyes. "A dance, Lady Lane?" A man bowed and held out his hand.

Looking wordlessly to Roy, I saw him nod then wander away to a group of sighing and swooning girls. "Alright, but I warn you I have two left feet." His hand on the small of my back, he led me to the middle of the dancers and as he put his palms on my waist, I placed my hands on his shoulders.

We swayed and a waft of something greeted my nose in a flurry of vanilla and brandy. He wore a mask, not one that covered your mouth but one you wear to a masquerade party. The mask was blood-moon red, matching his suit and tie. "I didn't know people like being anonymous at Balls. Or is it just something you do?" I teased as he swirled me around.

"I like to think it's a style." He answered, his voice low but not unpleasant.

Gazing up at him I told him, "Well, it is certainly a look." A playful smile grazed his lips and he put his hand up to my hair to stroke a strand away from my face. Grabbing his hand, I pushed it away.

He stopped swaying and stared at me. I gave him a death glare back. "You're not like many women You have a masculine soul that I can see as clearly as day." Looking over his shoulder, I spotted Roy surrounded by giggling, squealing ladies, fanning themselves and becoming quite hysterical. He was smiling a grin

I had not seen in weeks. It was genuine, a smile only happiness could summon.

I thought of Roy when I chose my next words and choose them carefully, I did. "Yes, I suppose I do? Is that a good thing?" I smiled.

"It's not what you should be, this is not who you should be." I felt tears, lava in my eyes as he spoke. "And what, good sir, should I be?"

"Married, raising children, cleaning, cooking, looking after your husband."

"I am 16, sir, and I shall never be your dream of a woman. If you want a kind of lady that would do that willingly than you shall spend your life alone." I spat, "Women don't need men, men need women." Leaning towards him, I put my face inches from his, "We are the flames, beautiful, light, pure. You are the moth; you are attracted to the flame and when you get too close, you get burnt."

Without wanting to waste another breathe on that man, I turned and glided towards Roy. "Roy, are you having fun?" I asked, sitting next to him on the table he sat on. The women watched me with interest and glancing at them I said, "Why do stare so?"

"Who are you to him?" One lady asked in a bright pink mermaid gown with hot pink lips and eyeshadow.

"His sister." They all breathed a sigh of relief. Roy caught my gaze and throwing his dazzling grin to the ladies he smirked, "Beg my pardon, ladies but I am afraid I must be off." They all begged him to stay and a couple kissed him on the cheek leaving lipstick stains. As we walked away, I turned him to face me, "C'm here, we cannot have you wandering around with the

ladies' lips imprinted on your skin can we mister?"
With the cloth I had taken from a table nearby, I wiped away the marks. "So, I guess Mr Unknown is either in a closet with his tongue cut off, or you found the kindness in your blackened heart and let the rat escape the trap."
"Something like that, Roy," I told him, picking up red wine from a table. We saw Roxanne dancing with the man that opens the door and I do think to this very day the way they were staring at each other was more than a look a boss gave to her worker.
"What do you think her problem is? Been picky on me ever since she met us in the alleyway." I asked him as I watched her under my eyelashes, not blinking.
"Come on Letty! She is obviously jealous of you, I mean look at you, who wouldn't. Tongue like a viper and a dress suited for a Goddess." Roy said. Leaning closer to me his nose scrunched up as he told me, "She doesn't even know my name." I smiled at that.
The man with the masquerade mask was in the corner of the room staring at me, his eyes never left my side. "Roy," I whispered taking a step closer to my brother and taking his hand in my free one, "Roy, that man, the one I was dancing with is staring at us," I nudged my head in his direction.
Roy glanced up then his palm on the small of my back he led me to the stairs. "Don't look," he hissed as I went to look over my shoulder. We got to the top of the stairs but then I saw Roy peer behind me, and he told me voice shaking, "Run."
I did not know where we were going but I just kept on running. My feet and Roy's had taken us back to our room. We stepped in and shut the door behind us. "Get the table!" I shouted and

together we pushed it against the door. Sighing, I collapsed into the chair next to the fire, head in my hands.

"I'm so stupid. I thought he was different but what does he want with us, following us here?" I whimpered. The door rattled and Roy and I seemed to freeze. "Roy?" I whispered. "Roy?" I said it a little bit louder and stood up to stand behind him. "Roy!" I shouted. Rattle. Rattle. Rattle. "Roy!" I shrieked, holding onto his arm.

A noise even more terrible joined it. The blade of a dagger scraped against the wall and a voice cackled, "Tabitha and Leo Swash? Daughter and son of Melony and Joseph Lane. Now that's not quite right, is it?" My face paled and I wanted to scream, to run.

"What do you want?" I sounded pathetic, like a young girl. The laughter that followed made me begin to shake and I had to close my eyes to stop the pitiful tears fall down my face.

"Name. Money. And I want you to come out," he told us, "Come out, come out wherever you are."

"We don't have your......." curses fell from my mouth, ".......money." I went to shout but Roy pushed me in front of him and covered my mouth. "Our names are..." he began, shakily, "Our names are Letty and Roy Lane."

"Good boy," the man coaxed as he twisted the nob ever so slowly. "Now open the door."

Teeth bit into Roy's fingers making him yelp in pain. "No! Go away! Go away!" I shrieked, "Leave us alone! We did nothing to you!"

"Wrong." He sang. "Open the door and no one gets hurt." Roy, me clinging to him, went to remove the table. We ran backwards as the door creaked open. There, the man in the masquerade mask stood.

He stalked into the room and sat on the bed. "Please make yourself comfortable." Roy plopped down on the chair. Raising his eyebrows at me. I felt my hands go clammy as they tightened into a ball. "I said sit." My legs stayed where they were. Hands wrapped themselves around my waist and pulled my downwards.

"Shh," Roy whispered in my ear. I leaned into him smelling his orange aroma. The man's sneer made me quake as my legs bounced up and down with my anxiety. Palms placed themselves on my knees and I heard my brothers rumbling voice, "What did we do?"

"You, Roy Lane, you bargained with me," he smiled viciously and then pointing at me said, "You, boasting about your fortune, told me you could give me 4 million pounds if you wanted to. You swore on your sister's life."

"I was drunk. I owe you nothing, not a penny, not a pound," Roy shouted back. Smirking, the man reached from inside of his jacket and withdrew a piece of paper. "Your signature to our agreement." He explained. I stood up. Roy called to me urgently, begging me to stay but I wouldn't listen. "Let me see that," I ordered one hand outstretched. Eyes looking down the length of my body handed me the paper. "Oh, yes, there it is! My brother's signature," I said maliciously.

Walking to the fire I turned to look at the man, "You tricked him, you kidnapped us, you killed Mami and Papi and you shall pay. You shall burn in your own fire. Me and everyone whose lives have been turned to hell because of you, shall watch you perish."

With that, I dropped the paper in the fire. The man stood and snarled, eyes flashing. "Signature or not you idiotic girl, I shall have my money." He stalked towards me knife in hand and grabbed me by my arm dragging me away. My screams were muffled as he gagged me with a cloth and held the blade to my neck.

Roy yelled and jumped to his feet, arms outstretched. "Stop! Stop! Do not hurt her!" Tears welled in my eyes, and I tried to break free but gasped as the knife dug into my flesh. I thought I felt blood but when the man withdrew the knife it was not dripping with the red liquid.

"Please..." Roy begged, "Please, she is all I've got." The man did not look sympathetic, and he just sneered. "Money then your sister."

"No, my sister then the money."

"I am the one with the knife, Roy." He reminded him. Roy nodded but did not move.

"You know what? I like you two, you're very entertaining so how about you two stay nice and safe here whilst I go and talk to the Lady of the house."

"What do you want with Roxanne?"

"Do not worry poppet, she is in good hands! The very best!" he left the room but not after he summoned a man. The very man who owned the strange store. "Ahh Mademoiselle you are well?" he asked in his French accent. I did not answer.

He went outside with the man whose face I had never seen but before they left, I called out to them, "Hey!" They looked at me, "Does that mean you're Leonardo Marvella?" He licked his lips and cackled, "Yes! Yes! Clever girl! Now sit tight and be good!"

The door swung shut. "Roy," I whispered.

"Letty."

"We have to leave."

"How?"

"The window?" I hurried to it, and it opened but when I leaned over, I sighed. "It's too far to jump."

"Why jump? Go and get dresses and suits as many as you can carry and hurry!" I did as I was asked and went to go and fetch them.

"Here," I handed them to him.

"Good. Tie this to the bed," I tied a lilac dress to the legs of the bed. "Keep on tying them." It took us minutes to knot everything together but finally a chain was made. We threw it out the window. "We will have to jump the last couple of metres. I'll go first and catch you when you fall."

"Wait let me get something!" I ran to the closet door and reappeared moments later with the sky-blue dress under my arm.

"What?" I asked, as Roy looked exasperatedly at me.

"Nothing." He blabbered. Walking to the window, he sat on it and climbed down. "Come on!" The doorknob was turning behind me. I swore, sat on the windowsill, and let go. Arms caught me. Without thinking I kicked of my heels and ran, Roy beside me.

"This was a bad! Bad! Bad! Idea!" I shouted. Gunshots came from the mansion, and I began to cry. "Roy!" I cried. He held my hand as we ran. Screaming joined the shots and I wanted to fall to the ground, curl in a ball and die. I sobbed as I picked up speed. When we were far enough away, on top of a hill overlooking the town, I fell to the floor and wailed.

We may not have pointed the guns, nor fired them, but we had just as well killed them. The grief, the overwhelming thoughts they suffocated me, like the sobs that got stuck in my throat. Roy just watched his own eyes dry. He seemed to have used all his tears. "Letty, we have to go," he told me. I just shook my head.

"I am sorry," I cried, "Mami, Papi forgive me," my hands clasped in prayer I looked up to the stars. Roy, taking my arms, dragged me away. I don't remember him taking me to the stables, I have no recollection of him putting me on one of the black horse's saddles and pushing the reins in my hands. I have no memory of riding through the trees and forgotten lands, I did not remember reaching a village and being helped down nor being guided to an inn and being coaxed into a bed.

I remember waking up though. Waking up and thinking everything had just been a dream but then I had pulled back the covers to see the dress, the dress I had thought to be a gown for a Queen.

The blue dress lay on the back of a chair next to the bed. I slowly got up and looked to my right, Roy lay next to me, his hair messy and clothes crinkled. Smiling I kissed his forehead then got out of bed, I detangled my hair the best I could with my fingers, its curls still stood strong. I pulled on the blue dress and watched myself in the mirror.

"Yes, you look beautiful now stop fawning over yourself," a grumpy voice came from the bed. Flushing, I turned to look at him. "Where did you take us?"

"The village of Courtley."

"Courtley? Surely you just made that up." I grinned. He just glowered at me, pulling the covers over his face. "What do we do now then?"

"What is there to do?"

"Try and find the money?" He huffed and grumbled at that. Then the most amazing thing fell from his mouth. A swear word.

"You swore!" I laughed.

"Yeah, well that money gets it."

"Just don't keep doing it, it is not a good look on you."

The last chance

Letty watched me intently for a while then smiled and told me, "Can we go and explore?" I returned her smile with a grin and answered, "I think we better."

The streets were almost empty apart from a couple of people walking by. There were many shops though, from little bakeries to large food shops. It was a cold day and the clothes me and Roy were wearing were not appropriate for such bitter weather. So, our first stop was a little building on the corner of the street where our inn was. It was a beige place and as soon as we entered something caught my eye. A turquoise blue, fur hemmed dress, standing proud and delightfully pretty on its rack. It was splendidly warm when I slipped it on.

I also donned a fur hat, white like snow and a long summer-day blue coat. I wore boots a blank white and gloves the colour of my eyes. Roy wore a thick jacket, long and black. He bought trousers as well and then he and me left. The lady at the till had given me a basket and I had placed our old clothes inside.

I shot a glance at an alleyway nearby, a shadow moved. It dashed away, further into the blackness. To go and follow it would be foolish, so I chose to ignore it and move on. As the day became closer to night, I felt, not for the second time, a figure in the darkness, not wanting to harm, but just watch. By now, Roy had felt the feeling too and when our eyes met, we both could not help but to let our curiosity win. We went down the alleyway. The further we went, the less sunlight there was and narrower the path.

"Roy, I don't like this. We should go back," I told him pulling on his sleeve.

"No. We cannot turn back now!" He was a fool for saying that but the fault for what happened next was mine for following him. There the figure stood. It was not just a shadow but a man. One covered in a black robe.

"Outrun the master? The man behind the mask?" The robe laughed. "He shall have his money. You shall give it to him before the moon that comes tonight turns to the sun." I glared at him, nostrils flaring and wanting so desperately for that man to fall dead. "And where are we supposed to find the money? Lying around in the streets with signs saying here is a free 4 million pounds?" I snarled. Roy grabbed my arm.

"We shall give it to you." The man stared at us for a while then nodded and was gone, lost to the shadows. Hands turned me to face them, "Letty you must go. Run. Nothing in this village is worth 4 million pounds, it is impossible to get. He will kill you." Tears I hated to see, fell down his cheek. I wiped them away, "Roy..."

"Please," he begged, "please, go." That decision I had to make right there was the hardest choice I had ever had to make. If I stayed, death would clutch me in his bony fingers, but I should not die alone but with my brother, the only family I had left. Leave and I escaped that skeletons wrath, but it would be the last time I would see Roy. I would rather die together.

"Roy." I said sternly, "Roy. If you think you can help me cheat death by sending me riding a horse far away from your murder scene then you would be wrong. Everyone dies, whether it is tomorrow, a week, years, or decades. Everyone's hourglass runs out, who are you to decide mine?"

"You can't understand." He moaned.

"Can't? Or don't? Tell me, help me understand. What pains your heart, sweet Roy?" I stepped forward and placed my forehead against his. His hands stroked my hair, and he sniffled before saying, "I made a promise to Papi. I promised him you would never be hurt that I would protect you." My heart melted at those words. All these years later and it still made my eyes swell to hear Roy talk about them.

"When?"

"It was the day when you had come home crying because your friends had been horrible to you and pulled your hair. You had sat on Papi's lap, by the fire. This was before Grandpa Eddie had become ill and he had sat by the flames as well. Mami had sent you to bed with a hot drink and Papi had called me down. Remember?" Roy choked on a sob, "he told me, my son, protect dear Letty from those people. Those cruel, bewitched people. He made me promise."

If I had known that before, would I have argued with Roy's pleads for me to run? No. I did not need protecting like a princess in a tower. If anything, I would be the knight. "No. I cannot." He looked like he was going to argue but watching my eyes narrow and brows raise, he sighed and took my arm.

"What are we to do then?" Roy asked.

"Keep on running? Run from the danger chasing us, enjoy the thrill, look forward to having a safe place to rest, to call home." Those words had fully transformed my life from one of a Lady almost sent to a boarding school, to a criminal on the run. We didn't talk about it at as we walked back to the inn, both of our minds had turned blank and sadness, perhaps a bit of excitement dug deeper into our hearts.

I found my mind less foggy the longer we walked, and I thought of Mami and her roses. Her sweet smelling roses. Papi used to buy her a bunch every week and how she loved them, talking to them and watering them like they were her children. Her aroma used to smell of the petals, her appearance so vividly like the flowers. Mami's dearest dress was a petal one, red like her favourite divine beauties.

The inn door opened, and we ambled in. A waft of smoke came at me, and I looked up. There in the corner of a room a girl sat kneeling at a fireplace trying to rub sticks together but only being able to make a small fire that was mostly smoke, before it burnt out in seconds of being lit. Her hair was like winter. Tresses dipped in its signature colours.

She reminded me of someone. Someone I could not quite put my finger on. I went over to her and sat next to her on the floor. "You're holding it all wrong." Moving her hands to the right position I told her, "Then you twist it in your palms." She did as I said and watched as a flame began to flicker, growing wide as it hungrily went from log to log.

"Do I know you?" I asked. The girl turned and answered me in a small voice, "No, I don't think so. You might be thinking of my sister." Roy stood behind me, his shadow falling over me and the girl. "Who is your sister?" The girl looked up.

"You do not know her? That's rare!" She smiled at me and brushing the bits of bark from her lap she beamed, "I am Harriet." Extending her hand to me, her eyes twinkled.

"Nice to meet you Harriet, I am Letty, and that's my twin brother Roy." Her eyes grew wide, before tears fell down her cheek. Startled I took her hand and said, "I am sorry was it something I said?"

"No," she sniffles, "No, it is just I had a twin too."

"Oh." I paused then added, "I am sorry."

"It's alright. He might be alive, but I very much doubt it." She wanted me to ask. I could see it by the way she glanced at me, then put her head down. I got up and sat on a chair across from the fire, I crossed my legs and asked, "What happened to him?"

Harriet's story

Letty sat; head held up high, as she questioned the girl. "What happened to him," she had asked. Harriet had taken a deep breath and told us everything, from the very beginning.

"It was just a couple of months ago, we had lived with our Mum and Dad. Dad was very ill, had a fever and was irritable. Mum had to work for the family. There were bills, school, food, and clothes to pay for. My Dad's condition got worse, and he ended up in a medical induced coma. My elder sister, Dorothy, got a job as an actress, she worked in plays and productions. She is a star, everyone in town knows her.

It was only me and my brother, Ethan, who saw her for what she was, an entitled brat. But she gave us money and we slowly paid for Dad's medical bills. We could even pay for small luxuries sometimes. My sister had grown a habit for gambling, she lost hundreds, sometimes thousands, weekly. No one knew apart from me; I was forbidden to tell a living soul. One night, Dorothy gambled with the wrong person. His name was Leonardo Marvella. He tricked her into owing him millions of pounds - she could not even pay half of it.

Angry as he was, he stole my brother away from us and took him far away. He must be terribly frightened, I told myself but no one else seemed to care apart from Dorothy and me. Mum saw it as one less mouth to feed and to pay for and Dad, well, if he saw the situation, I don't know what he would think of it all.

Mum, forgetting her past life of bankruptcies, lost all of our money on drugs and drinks. Sorry for what she had done,

Dorothy took us away to here, Courtley. We have been here for roughly a month. She works here but is ill today, she is in bed at home and sent me here to work instead."

It was a heart melting story, one that made me cry inside. Letty who had kept a neutral face all the way through, wiped a tear from her cheek. "The boy, he had hair like yours." It wasn't a question but a statement, a fact. "Yes." Harriet solemnly replied.

"I saw him. We were taken by that man as well. I saw him in a courtyard," Letty's voice broke as she told her. Harriet gazed up at her with eyes that had been mirrored in her brothers. It was a look that made her eyes glazed over with confusion. "I am truly sorry." I spoke for the first time, and the girl smiled up at me.

My sister stood, kissed Harriet on both cheeks and whispered something into her ear before we both left to go to our room up the stairs.

Later that evening, Letty left to go and ask the girl for some bags, whilst I stayed and waited. A soft knock came from the door, "Come in." Harriet's face poked round the door.

"Letty was looking for you." I told her turning my back and walking to the window, to shut it. Harriet did not respond, and I heard breathing, rapid and uneven behind me. "Harriet?" I looked at her. She was standing there, tears streaming down her cheeks and sobbing, eyes wild. "Help me! Please help me!" Harriet ran towards me putting her arms around my waist.

I just stood there holding the girl I barely knew as she wailed, "You mustn't tell Letty! You mustn't! You mustn't!"

"Tell her what?" I was baffled.

She leaned closer and whispered, "He will kill me and Dorothy if we don't. You must help us. Oh, please, help us!"

"But how? How can I help you?"

"Kill him! You're a man. He prefers men. Try to reason with him." Idiotic child. Reason with the man who wants my neck on a silver platter? Only an insane person would do that! I shook my head and watched as she writhed and wailed.

I crouched down to her level and told her simply, "I cannot. Neither shall I try." Straightening up I added, "Between you and me if anyone in this world was going to kill that man. It would be my sister, Letty with the blood on her hands."

"I cannot find......" The door opened as Letty entered, "Oh. There you are. Are you alright?" Letty's soft expression fell over her face as she smiled at Harriet. The girl nodded and sniffed. Then, she looked at me. Her cold, fire piercing eyes glared at me. "I did nothing," I told her. She stopped her frown and told the girl, "Come on, let's get you back downstairs."

Taking the girls shoulder, Letty guided her out of the room. For many minutes, I continued to stare at the door until it opened and the furious voice of my dear sister hit me, "What happened then?" I knew Harriet had told me not to tell Letty but how could I not?

There was swearing, quite a bit of swearing after that. "What should we do?" She asked.

"Um, sorry? What is there to do?"

"Well, we cannot just leave her here to die, can we?" Letty's scowl returned. Her eyebrows raised when I failed to answer. "She is a child."

"And last time I checked, we were children as well, you don't see people helping us, do you?"

"Roxanne did. That little girl did."

I scoffed, "What did she do?"

"She helped us see we are not the only ones in the world who are scared of death because of him. She told us we are not alone."

"Does it matter?" She sounded ridiculous. Not alone? We are, she was just too blind to see it. "I'm leaving!" Turning heel, she stormed off, slamming the door behind her. I sighed as I fell on to the bed. I just can't do anything right, can I?

Hours had passed and Letty had still not returned. I kept on looking out of the window to try and see tresses of ginger curls walking by. It must have been midnight. Letty was still nowhere to be seen and I found myself drowsy with sleep. Closing my eyes, I prayed to myself that when I woke up my sister would be sleeping beside me.

A fighting chance

I am afraid that was the last time you shall read the words from my darling Roy. The story, our story, shall now be passed on, for only me to explain. So, like my brother told you he waited hours that night for me to return but instead of giving in to my pathetic anger, I kept away. Sauntering around the alleyways and streets.

It was the wind that howled and whipped my hair that night. I felt alive. Free. I could have gone back and prevented what was to come but I didn't. Fury blinded my better judgment and it felt good to be mad! Not fearful or running for my life. As I walked, I saw through a crimson shade and stormed down an alleyway.

I yelped!

Hands covered my mouth and pulled me inside of a shop. They shushed me as they hit my head. My ears rang and I stayed motionless and limp in the persons arms as they lifted me up and walked out. I did not know where they were taking me but I held my tongue. A door was opened, he stepped inside, and I remember his knee hitting my back as he stalked upstairs.

Again, a door was swung open. I was sat on the floor and somebody lying on the bed opposite me, snored softly. I cried out. "Roy!" He slept, without knowing, without fearing the figure standing at the bottom of his bed.

"You are not going to get me money with that boy around are you sweetheart?" The man rasped.

"Please. No! Not Roy! Anyone but Roy!" He just laughed and pulled a knife from inside his cloak. Pointing it at my brother he smirked, "Anything you want to say?"

I wanted to shout curses at him until my throat grew raw, but nothing fell out and I just stared in horror at the knife in his hand. Roy turned in his sleep. My brother. My darling, sweet brother. Seeing through watery eyes I told him, "Why? Why go to such length for money?"

"I don't answer to you Letty Lane, my God, how you remind me of *her*." I gulped. I knew who *her* was. "You have the same look in your eyes, and you talk with a mouth full of snake's venom.

He raised the knife. "Roy!" I shrieked. "Roy, wake up! Wake up!" His eyes fluttered and he slowly opened them. "Roy!" He shot awake! Staring at his fate, he whispered, "No, oh God please no." Turning to me, Roy shouted, "Run!" I heard his yell and jumped up.

The knife did its bidding.

It was quick and deadly. Roy, my twin brother, lay unmoving. Ghostly white, blood soaking his shirt. I felt the scream leave my lips, felt hands pulling me away, out of the room and down the stairs. Horror left me speechless but I fought against the grip of the hands holding me. "Letty!" I was shocked to see that it was Harriet holding onto me. I stopped.

Feet were running towards the stairs. Grabbing Harriet, we both made for the door just managing to miss the knives thrown at us. Cold sweat trickled down my neck as I sprinted to an alleyway, yanking Harriet with me.

He was dead. Roy was dead. Lost to the world of the living, Roy now served the Gods in the Heavens. My brother had fulfilled his promise to our Papi and may his blessed pure soul rest in peace now. His death was not in vain. I shall avenge him. The vendetta between me and that scoundrel Leonardo Marvella appeared to have blackened my heart that night.

I feared, never again I would smile or laugh. Feel the heat on my cheeks and feel my insides flutter. To cry would show weakness but who was I stop them falling down my cheeks? They were like endless streams of my bitter guilt and unmendable despair.

With a little girl clinging onto me, we ran away from the inn. That god awful inn. A carriage nearby with a driver sat at the front was at the end of the road we were sprinting down. Climbing into it I gasped, "Go, please go!" Seeing our faces, he nodded and rode as fast as was wise on the road.

Looking behind us, I saw a man standing there, a mask covering his face, a bloody blade in his hands. I collapsed, breathing heavily as I turned back around. No words were said between me and Harriet. She was sitting there, her eyes wild and her hand over her heart. I opened my arms. She shuffled closer placing her head on my shoulder and leaning against me. Putting my arm around her, I began to sing.

It was a song about roses. Sweet smelling roses and the dead. A beautiful song with words with great meaning weaved together to make a melody. A melody that sang of how the dead is never left behind and how they are never really gone. As Harriet's eyes fluttered closed, I stroked her hair rocking back and forth. The symphony of my voice soothed her to a slumber.

I looked at the seat opposite me where a Roy shaped hole was missing. "You alright love?" the driver asked, "Do you want me to get someone for you?" The child in my arms shifted, shaking in the cold. "Yes. Do you know where Dorothy lives? She is the sister of this girl."

"Ay, that I do. Works in the only inn in town, used to be famous, she did." He changed the horse's direction, down an empty street. The moon hung in the sky in front of us, the clock ticking away. He stopped in front of a bungalow. It had vines freely growing up it, frost lined the floor and the windows. I hopped down, leaving Harriet in the carriage and without knocking opened the door.

A waft of cherry floated towards me. The room, though it had no fire, was warmer than outside. I made my way down a tiny corridor to a door shut closed; I heard sniffling coming from the room. I rapped on the door and a weak voice answered me, "Harriet?"

"I am afraid not." I stepped inside and saw a girl, not much older than me. With silky black hair lying around her wearing a nightdress. "Please, you must come with me, your sister is in a carriage outside. We don't have much time. Bring some food, warm clothes. We must be off!"

She asked no questions, but slid out of bed and padded to her closet pulling out trousers, a blouse and a long dark green coat. I left and headed to the kitchen that was only five steps away and went through the cupboards looking for bread or cans of food. Anything that would last long I put in a bag I found under the sink.

"You wear men's clothes?" in that time if anyone asked that question, they would say it in disgust or sneered it. I did no such thing. I said it in surprise and with a warm smile. Without me explaining what was going on, we left that bungalow and went to the carriage. Harriet had curled up into a ball and slept fitfully.

Dorothy put her sister on her lap, resting her chin on Harriet's head. I sat opposite them watching how close they were. When the wheels were rolling again and the horses taking us far away, Dorothy started to ask questions. "Who are you and what on Earth is going on?"

"I am Letty, Letty Lane." I explained everything from when I had been captured, with my brother, to that very moment. I remember it as if it had been yesterday. She had sat so silent throughout it all, looking at her sister, gazing up at me when I tumbled on my words, or my voice broke. She nodded and smiled sadly at me like she knew everything that had happened to me in those last few weeks.

I wish Roy had been there to hold my hand as I wept, tucking my knees up to my chest ignoring the driver's questions, "Was I alright?" To answer him, no I wasn't. I had never cried like I did then, so many tears fell, I am surprised I did not drown in them. There seemed no point to carry on, who was I doing it for? Me? I should have been the one with the knife in my chest, not Roy.

The drive was long and I had no energy to ask where we were going. "You can sleep," Dorothy told me, "I will keep watch." I was going to argue, maybe swear at her, but drowsiness had me in its clutches and the last thing I saw was the face of little Harriet.

Life, as I never knew

Hands shook me and I heard someone whispering, "Letty, wake up." I opened my eyes. The face of Dorothy stood in front of me, Harriet beside her clutching her sister's hand and watching me with large eyes. The carriage had stopped moving and we were somewhere surrounded by trees and fields as large as small villages.

"How much?" I asked the driver. He smiled and turning his body to face me he told me, "It is on the house. I don't charge people who are running from danger." He winked at me, "Now you look after yourself love." Me, Harriet, and Dorothy watched as the carriage ambled away.

I looked up at the sky and realised with a pang of fear, morning had come. This was the time we... I was supposed to hand over the money. Without turning back, I started to walk. The earth beneath my feet was uneven in patches and I felt the puffs of the wind on my face, tasted the dryness of my mouth and yearned for water to soothe my sore throat.

The faces of the trees seemed to laugh at me, their gnarly lines a sneer. No animals fluttered or went by, the world was as empty as I felt. I heard the sisters behind me talking in hushed whispers and I wanted so desperately to do the same with Roy.

The strides of my steps grew quicker as I spread out the distance between us. 'Alone' is what the world wanted me to be, so alone I shall be. Why wouldn't the mud beneath my feet trip me?

I was so entranced in the scene that replayed before me that I did not hear feet running behind me, did not feel as a cold hand held mine. "Letty?" Harriet stood next to me, something cupped in her hand. "What is it?" I asked. A necklace lay in her palm. It was a divine red, and it reflected my face as I took it and held it up to the sun. It was the colour of Mami's roses, the colour of Roy's blood.

I was left speechless but when I did speak it was a tiny voice that left my mouth, "Thank you." She beamed and called to her sister, who came to us, and I saw Dorothy's sad smile painted on her face.

We walked for hours — cold, bitter wind fighting against us. Dorothy had picked up Harriet when she had begun to slow down, and the girl had rested her head wearily on her sister's shoulder and shut her eyes. "What are we to do now?" Dorothy asked. I shook my head and responded, my voice still weak, "We could perhaps find shelter. Night comes quickly when you so desperately need it to stay day."

There weren't many choices on where to stay — there were no human inhabitants and all that lay around us was a void of greenery and white frost. We settled under a willow tree its crooked branches acted like a roof. "Harriet told me about your brother." Dorothy said. "I am sorry."

"Yeah, well, there is nothing anyone can do to bring him back." I huffed. Turning my back on them, I huddled into a ball, tears streaming down my face. I slept.

I awoke. Morning had not yet come as the sky still donned its black sea. My back and arms felt stiff from the rock-hard earth and I groaned as I sat up.

The world had vanished in a white sheet. It lay on the trees, hiding them. It coated the grass, leaving it a wide unceasing stretch of penetrating coldness. I could have sat and looked around me as long as it would take to melt, as it really was a beautiful scene, of icicles and frost. I knew, if I had slept any longer, I may have never woken up.

A flickering ember withered on top of the twisted, crooked sticks. It was a dying flame and stood a pathetic fight to beat of the bitterness of the world surrounding us. I saw the girl whose hair blended into the snow and her sister hugging her as they tried to stay warm. Harriet's hair was blown softly as she breathed out and I watched as her dress became patterned with tiny snowflakes that fell between the gaps in the branches above us.

Dorothy twitched and huddled closer to little Harriet as a gust of wind hit her back. Both of their lips were blue with cold and I was fearful they would never see another day. I went to them and shook them. Dorothy sighed and tried to open her eyes to find them glued shut. "Here." I gently prised them open.

Unmoving, Harriet lay like she had been frozen stiff with ice. "Harriet?" Dorothy said. "Harriet?" She prodded her sister and shook her but to no avail. The little figure did not awake, and she slept peacefully on. Her sister's movements became frantic as she tried to make her at least stir. Harriet's hair in front of her face did not move, her chest did not go up and down with the rhythm of her lungs.

I left; I got up and I left her there, holding Harriet to her chest as she wept. The willow tree called to me, "Come back," its branches whispered as the wind hit them with its force. I had no destination but I just kept on wandering. Wandering far away from that dead little girl and her grieving sister.

Two lives had been taken with no justice and for what? What

cause? Leonardo shall pay for the lives he has taken; he shall die a painful death.

I stumbled over hills and rocks, I foundered hours later, collapsed on the soft floor of snow, and cried. Cried the tears that grief summons. Death watched me and laughed. Cackling as he saw how much pain and suffering he had caused me. I crawled to a sturdy oak tree and leaned my forehead against it. Fumbling with my hands, I clutched at a rough, thin twig and peering up, I engraved Roy's name into the bark.

It wasn't perfect - it was clumsy, and the letters were not connected. "I hate you." I whispered, trying not to blink to stop the pathetic tears crusading down my face. "When Mami died and Papi, you comforted me. We comforted each other." Sniffing, I wiped my nose with the soft fabric of my sleeve and breathed, "Now, I am alone. Alone and so lonely." My voice broke.

I felt the world crashing down, felt my heart break into millions of unmendable pieces and I begged, I screamed for the floor to swallow me whole. He was gone. Taken from the world, his life, his friends. Me.

His name engraved in the tree stood a reminder of his sacrifice. It wasn't enough, nothing anyone could do would be enough! I leaned against the trunk; my back flushed against the roughness. "Roy, no one living knows what it is like to be ……" I couldn't say it. To speak it out loud would mean making it official, for it to become reality, not just a terrible, terrible nightmare.

I closed my eyes and tilted my face to the sky. The clouds mourned too as they cried their tears; the wind howled its mellow thrum of song, and the trees shook with their sobs as they swayed. "Is it true?" I wailed, "Is it true there is a heaven?"

No one answered me and I felt my insides fall into each other as I stood up. I opened my mouth and shrieked. I shrieked and screamed until my throat was raw and the tears fell like shattered glass hitting the floor. Falling on my knees, I sobbed and cried but did not scream again. "Roy. Roy. Brother..." I wept as I leant forward and placed my forehead on the bark.

Never again would I hear his voice, smell the aroma of orange, or be loved for the bitter words of my tongue.

I gazed at the words, Roy Lane. They became blurrier the longer I stared at them. "I will kill him, brother." I told him, "I promise I will."

I felt the lump building in my throat but pushed it down. I didn't want to cry anymore - it is not what Roy would have wanted. Crouching down, I kissed the imprint of my brother's name and muttered, "Farewell Brother. Say hello to Mummy and Daddy for me if you see them, won't you?"

Getting up, I walked away. Each step felt like betrayal, each breath felt like a curse. Roaming around, I saw smoke billowing high into the air from between trees nearby. I made my way towards them, stepping carefully so as to not break a stick, drawing attention to myself.

Laughing and chatting began to get louder the closer I got to the smoke. I could see them now. Three people sat over a fire, passing around flasks, and eating what looked like fish. Hiding behind a tree, I watched them. There were two boys, with a girl sitting between them. They were all around my age, I think, and they smiled at one another, kidding around.

One of the boys had blonde curls and had green, emerald eyes. He had a friendly face and when he smiled, a dimple blossomed on his right cheek. The other one looked more tuff. He had a scar across one of his eyes and his greasy black hair was slicked back into a ponytail.

The girl had blonde locks and shared a resemblance with the boy with green eyes. Jokily, she punched the boy with the black hair and laughed, her nose scrunching up. She must have sensed my eyes, as she stared at them. She looked up and met my gaze. I stepped back and heard her call out, "Look! A girl!" The boys peered at me too, they both stood and advanced towards me.

Turning, I sprinted away. I heard them shouting and heard feet scrambling after me. I shot a glance behind me and saw the two boys chasing close behind. They were fast but I was faster, with each step grew a bigger distance between us. I hid behind a tree to catch my breath and sank downwards sitting on my heels.

"Where did she go?"

"I don't know. I'll look over here. You look over there." Someone was approaching but I had no energy to run away. The boy with curls stood before me, I leaned backwards pushing against the tree. "Here, Axel!" the boy shouted. The scar faced man joined him in his ominous position staring down at me.

Axel took a step closer to me. I yelped and shuffled away. "You're scaring her!" the blonde boy said, putting a hand on Axel's shoulder, "Are you here alone?" I nodded. The girl was there as well her face donned a soft expression. "Who are you?"

"Letty Lane."

Three pairs of eyes blinked back at me. "Oh, Josh, we cannot leave her here to freeze to death. I can tell you right now she is a sweetheart! I can see it on her face." Sighing, Josh took a step towards me and held out his hand. Not knowing what to do, I simply stare at it. "You can trust us," The girl said gently.

I let Josh pull me up and guide me back the way we had come. "I am Bianca." The girl informed me taking my hand in hers. "Good grief! You are freezing!" She rubbed my fingers in her hands. "Darling, you are so cold you could be made out of ice!"

When we got back to the fire, she sat me down on a log and instructed me not to move. "It is a horrible time of the year but beautiful. Don't you think?" She did not wait for my reply before rattling on, "Now why are you here?" Telling strangers my story seemed a habit now. The boys watched me, mouths falling open. Once I had finished, Bianca hurried to me and pulled me into a bone crushing hug, "You poor lamb! Oh, you must stay with us! We are heading north to a town we hope to stay at!"

She turned to Axel and Josh, "Can we keep her? Please. She is so cute, and I am so bored of having no girls here! Oh please!" She pinched my cheeks, and I felt the smile that had been lost slowly edging its way onto my lips. "See?" Bianca said, exasperated. Josh laughed and nodded, Axel just grunted and turned to the fire.

Releasing my cheeks, she handed me a cup and ordered, "Drink up love." The liquid tasted of nothing, but it soothed my throat and warmed my insides. I looked up to find Josh was still gazing at me. "What?"

"Who is this Leonardo Marvella chap?"

"The most dangerous, murderous person to ever walk this planet, and free he does walk. He killed my Mami and Papi, my twin brother and he just as well killed Harriet." I stared at the cup, not meeting Josh's gaze.

He said no more but shuffled around to talk to Axel. Everyone seemed so excited about going north, it seemed the lantern at the end of a very, very, very long, very dark hallway.

As evening drew nearer, everybody began to slow down. There was no wandering around restlessly by the fire or collecting more wood to feed the flames. They sat down on their logs and muttered quiet conversations to themselves. I stayed away, not talking or meeting anyone's gaze.

To stumble upon such kind people in a world full of ruffians was a miracle. A blessing. Perhaps the Gods were not so cruel and unrefined as I had once thought. I knew nothing of the North. Was it a snow wonderland where it was always winter? Or a desert with a scathing sun overlooking the parched ground?

"Letty?" I looked up. Bianca was offering me her hand. I took it and she led me to a patch of earth that no snow or twigs lay sprawled over. She left and came back with a knitted blanked under her arm. She lay it on the floor and told me, "We shall sleep here. We move at first light."

Axel and Josh slept on the other side of a tree that was behind us. The rustling and low murmurs was what I listened to, as I settled down. I lay on my back and looked up the sky above me. The tree's naked branches stretched out of its thick trunk, the moon a glistening ball in the night. Soon I heard the gentle snoring of Bianca and knew the world was sleeping.

I wondered what had happened to Dorothy. Maybe I should have gone back to see if she still wept there but then I would have had to see Harriet's body. I have not yet seen or been told what had become of the famous sister of the dead twins and in my restless nights that is the one thought that drifts into my mind.

So, I lay failing sleep next to a girl I knew nothing of that night. When the ache to do something became an unbearable yearning,

I got up, careful to not awake Bianca. With the people I had spent the last few hours with, I think I knew what kind of people they were.

Axel was the moth, for no reason apart from the fact that he was very unlikeable so why would anybody want to be attracted to him? And sweet Bianca would be the flame, people would try and get close to her as she even emanated happiness and her kindness. Now Josh, he is the difficult one. He is neither the flame nor a moth. Why? You shall see later.

Trekking through the snow, I made my way out onto the fields and breathed in the cold night air. It tickled my nose and I felt its chilly wave going down my body to my lungs. To me, it seemed the vicious viper had lost its tongue. It seemed very long ago I had spoken in different languages now all I had spoken for days was Roy's language – English.

Just to test the words waiting to be used, I spoke in Spanish. It was fast but not as fast as I spoke in French. I cannot remember what I said to the night. I remember it replying though. The trees its hands, the stars its eyes, the snowflakes its tears.

"What are you doing?" A cold, angry voice came from behind me. I wheeled around. Axel stood there; he did not blink; he did not move. I answered him and when he glared at me under his frosty gaze, confusion but a slither in his expression. I blushed with embarrassment. I had unwisely spoken in my Spanish.

"Bianca has a good heart, do not betray her otherwise I will kill you." Ok. Do not mess with Axel, note taken. Turning back, he paused and a flit of something gentle swayed in his eyes as he spoke, "You should sleep." Then his cold-eyed stare was back.

"I cannot. How can I? People I love are dead because of me and I am permitted to sleep?" He gazed at me and shaking his head said, "No. You need sleep. You are not their murderer but their 'revenger'."

A boy after my own heart. Their 'revenger' not their murderer. Yes, I liked that a lot.

I did not return to Bianca for a long while. I sat down on a boulder and pondered. How was I to kill Leonardo Marvella? It should be excruciatingly slow. Burnt to the stake? His nails ripped off one-by-one? Drowning him? Watching his money burst into flames?

All suitable punishments, I think!

A thought occurred to me, one that made my tongue turn dry. Since when did I plan people's demises? I was a girl, a 16-year-old girl, a teenager. A child. I was supposed to be at a boarding school with friends and teachers I hated and loved. Instead, I was there, a nobody, with people I did not trust.

I returned to the girl curled up asleep on the floor but before I shut my eyes, I saw Axel, smiling at me before he disappeared behind the tree that separated us.

Hope, staring at me in the face

The next day to greet me, was yet again a dismal display of snowy skies and bitter cold weather. My first time travelling north was oddly exciting for me. I had a destination, a plan. No one talked as we tramped through thick snow, only when we had travelled far enough that the tips of the trees that had surrounded us, as we had slept, could not be seen, the buzz of conversation started.

"What are you going to do when you get to the North, Letty?" Bianca asked, her nose pink and ears a matching shade. "I don't know, "I shrugged, "what are you going to do?"

"I want to stay with my sister. She is a Lady in the palace, she works for the King's wife."

I frowned, "You mean the Queen?" She shook her head and shifting her bag from one shoulder to another told me, "She is not a Queen in fact she isn't really Royalty at all." She paused then continued, "She wasn't born into the role, the King fell in love with her, and God knows how he managed to convince his parents to let him wed her. They were all, 'You must marry Royal blood kind of people'. But he managed it."

The boys in front of us had stopped talking to listen. "Me and Rebecca, when I wasn't travelling north, used to send each other letters. Apparently it isn't a healthy relationship. He has a lot of illegitimate children and a handful of mistresses as well!"

"But she doesn't leave him, does she B?" Josh chimed in, it seemed he had heard the story many times before.

"No, she didn't! She stayed with him; you see Rebecca told me

that she hasn't loved the King for years, but she is well looked after there and has a right heart for drinking. So the tale goes!"
We climbed a slope of a hill, the snow slush beneath us.
"Well, truth be told Bianca, I don't know what I will do when I get there."
"In that case you must stay with me!" Bianca laughed and linked arms with me cheeks a healthy shade of flush pink. Axel turned around and gave me a stare that made me shiver.
It was midday by the time we reached a village. It was a small one lined with little, sweet cottages. When we walked across a pebbled street, the waft of fresh air still strong in our noses, Josh led us to a pub. "We should get a drink, lighten the heart and freshen the soul."
The warmth of the pub comforted us as we stepped in from the chilly day. The man behind the bar had his back turned to us and he barked to Josh who was trying to get his attention, "Alright! Alright! Calm down!"
Axel ordered us drinks, then we settled in chairs by the fire in the corner of the room. "Here you are." A girl placed an overflowing beverage in front of Bianca. She handed Axel and Josh their drinks then turned to me, "Here you go."
My drink looked strange. It didn't smell right and had no froth like the other three. I gingerly went to take a sip, but the drink was slapped out of my hands before I could even put it halfway to my lips. "It has been poisoned!" Josh bellowed. He glared at Axel, "Why do you want them to kill her?"
"What?"
"Why do you want to kill her?"
"No mate, you got it all wrong, I didn't make the drinks," Axel

calmly said. Josh snorted and stormed out of the pub. On the verge of tears, Bianca screamed for him to come back but he did not listen. It can't have been him, he can't have tried to poison me, he had no reason too.

"Letty, I swear I had nothing to do with this. Believe me." I looked up at him and saw a tear roll down his cheek. "I am sorry, but I don't know who to trust anymore." Getting up, I walked around to Bianca and gave a quick hug before saying, "I'll see you again." I stepped out once more into the freezing air and walked, head down, hands in my pockets away.

Why must everything be so terribly confusing? When you are sure you are safe then the fire burns out, leaving you alone once more? Heading north might not be a bad idea but I should think it over after some sleep.

"Letty!" I turned around, Bianca was hurrying towards me, arms wildly motioning me to stop. "I am coming with you!" She said undeterred by the frown playing on my face. Arguing would be futile, so I let her follow me, a bubbly smiling child at a runner's heel. The village was a deserted iceberg, each house a home for the cold that had moulded its thick layer of ice on top and around them.

I swore to the Gods in the skies. I swore so loudly that the world covered its ears, the wind picked up pace trying to cover up my screams of forbidden words. It tried, with no avail; my tongue countered its deafening howl, its shrieking, its orders to stop. My eyes streamed with the tears I had promised myself not to shed.

I wiped then away as they turned to angry tears. "Come now! Stop your crying and keep walking." Bianca chided, pushing me forward. Stumbling, I asked her, "How long till we get to the

North?"

"Not long. A day's journey. Sweetheart, this will be over, it will be a mere memory in your life, this isn't the end." Bianca smiled; benevolence soothed into her words. Perhaps I got lucky after all. I linked my arms with her and looked up into her twinkling eyes. I returned it with the lifted corners of my mouth.

We got to a church that sat with dignity and clothed as fine as to have diamonds and glass placed in neat rows on top of it. It smelt strongly of something I could not quite put my finger on. "Beeswax." Bianca told me. The door was unlocked, and we creaked it open to enter.

"Isn't that strange? Normally, people would take pride in such a beautiful building," Bianca whispered as her voice echoed around the room. It was spacious and the most decorated church I had seen. I do not know how such a small village built such a thing.

"Oh, Letty, look!" Two stone statues lying on a platform had words imprinted on one side. "Maria Carter, aged 6, and Cousin Lucas Beckett, aged 8, were some of the many people that died in a terrible fire."

"Horrible." I gasped.

"Truly horrific," Bianca confirmed, moving on and reading the other scripted memorials. Walking to the other side of the church, I read out loud the sign next to a stone boy with a scar across his eye. He stood, arms by his side, in scruffy clothes. I fell backwards and landed on my back, scrambling away from him like he had a knife in his hands. Someone put their hands on my shoulder and panicking, I turned around.

"It is just me! Just me!" Bianca exclaimed, crouching down next to me, "What is the matter? You look as though you have seen a ghost."

"I fear that I have." Bianca cocked her head to one side and gazing upwards read. She too collapsed leaning against me breathing rapidly. "No…" She moaned, "No…" There, 30 years or so younger, stood Leonardo Marvella. He looked innocent, like he wouldn't hurt a fly, like all he wanted was some nice food and to play with his friends on the street.

"It says he died in the fire as well."

"But he didn't. He lived."

"Yes, that's right, I lived."

Fight or flight

We both wheeled around and there, in flesh and blood, he stood.
"You!" I spat.
"I!" He threw back his head and laughed. "You Lane's never learn, do you?" Me and Bianca both stood and glared at him. Strips of black linen were weaved around his head, leaving holes for his ears, mouth, and eyes.

I froze and stared at him. His hand went to reach inside his jacket but before he could pull out a gun, I grabbed hold of Bianca and pushed her towards the door. He smirked, a wicked glint playing in his eyes. I got so far as the door myself before I heard the cock of the gun. I slowly turned to see it pointing at my face.

"I do not have your money."

"Then you shall pay." I closed my eyes waiting for the quick blow but instead, fire shot up from my leg. I shrieked as I collapsed. Redrawing my hand, I saw blood staining my fingers and palm. Someone dragged me away as I fought and screamed.

"How do you always find me?" I groaned, rocking back and forth from my agony.

"What is the fun in telling you?" Smiling, he kneeled in front of me. Lifting my head with the tip of his gun he told me, "I am going to tell you a story." Leonardo cackled once more before beginning, "I was 10 years old when my parents were taken from me. The same people who killed them, started the fire. The fire burnt the village down and it was 5 years later when they finished rebuilding a quarter of it."

He let my head drop as he stood and circled me, gun poised. "They only needed to build that much because everyone else was dead, they didn't need houses." Suddenly, the gun went off. This time hitting me on my arm. I reeled and gasped for air.

"My house had gone up in flames. I was the boy everyone had forgotten, the boy no one had gone back to save. I jumped from the window and saw the village rejoicing not because of me, their backs were turned on me, no, they were celebrating because another person had escaped the blaze. No-one had noticed me. No-one cared." Snarling, he took a dagger from his sleeve and climbed on top of me, pinned me down on the floor.

Tracing my neck with the blade, he whispered in my ear, "You have no idea what it is going to happen to you." Desperate to get away, in vain, I punched him and bit him. It wasn't going to end like that, I was determined to not die! I swore and cursed, clawing at the linen hiding his face.

I told him, "You can try and escape your past, you can try and outrun it but you shall always be the boy no one loved." Marvella roared and lifting the knife, plummeted it downwards, digging it into my chest.

I didn't scream. I didn't cry.

I looked to my right and saw him. Roy. He was a pale wispy blue figure, he turned and gazed at me. The smile I adored grazing his lips. I felt the chill his presence made, felt the coldness seep through my veins as he took my hand.

His eyes fell on something walking towards us, I moved my head to see what it was and... a figure with a rose held in her ghostly fingers glided towards me. Her dress like red petals. She kneeled in front of me and stroked my hair, "My brave, brave girl. My beautiful, beautiful daughter. Oh, my darling how much I missed you."

"Mami..." I croaked, she laughed and kissed my forehead.

"My baby girl, your time is not done."

Shaking my head, I gasped, tears crusading down my cheeks, "No, I want this to end. This must be my end." This time it was my Mami's turn to shake her head.

"No. No my sweet, sweet Letty, your time is not done." The smell of roses was so comforting and familiar that my body relaxed, my vision went blurry, and my mind was slowly becoming at ease. "Violetta." Her voice was louder now, clearer, "You have spent your life since me and you Papi's death thinking about revenge. It blackens the heart, baby, it changes people. Do not kill him for revenge but to save others from him."

She wasn't listening. I was done. I wanted to be free. "Letty," It was Roy who spoke. "Letty, you can do this." Looking at him stars twinkled in my line of view.

"But I have already lost..." I told him.

He smiled and squeezed my hand, "I can heal you. All I need is your consent."

It was a short while before I spoke, "There will be others to kill him. Others that are better equipped and braver." Roy sighed and my Mami kissed my forehead again.

"It is your choice my darling, but I know if you turn away now you shall never rest in peace." How did she know that? She hadn't been with me when I saw people die. She doesn't know that someone had tried to poison me. That I witnessed a little girl perish because of winter's freezing breath.

"Letty, you know it to be true. You know what he has done, if you let him live for a week more, hundreds of countless innocent lives shall be lost." Roy told me. I laughed as I shook my head, tears crusading down my face.

I looked up to where Leonardo had been minutes before. "This isn't real. I am dreaming, this is all in my head."

"Of course, this is all happening in your head Letty, but why does that mean it is not real?" My brother winked at me, and I nodded whilst saying, "Alright. I shall kill him." If only I knew what those words had done. If only I knew what was to come.

Mami lent forward and whispered, "We will watch you. My darling girl, me, Roy, and your Papi shall watch you." She picked up her rose she had placed on the floor as she stood. I looked to Roy then back at Mami, but she had disappeared.

"Letty."

"Roy?"

"Letty, I shall heal you then you shall have to go back to reality. No time has passed there. I shall stay with you." He put his hands around the handle and drew it out. I was numb — I felt nothing at all. Smiling, he hovered his hands over the wound and blue dust fell from his palm. My chest glowed, illuminated by a white light. Before the brightness lessoned, I felt my eyes close.

I awoke to the heavy breathing of my 'almost' murderer. "How? How is this possible?" He was staring at my chest where it was still bloody, but the wound had healed, not even leaving a scar. The knife had vanished, we were both unarmed. Cackling wildly, he dragged me to my feet and sneered, "Come on then, let's see how brave you are when I beat you senseless, you witch!"

He walked slightly away from me. His stance tense with knuckles ready to throw a punch. I simply stood there waiting for him to make his first move. He knocked the wind out of me with a blow to the chest and kneeing me in the stomach, he sent me gasping on the floor.

"Pathetic," he spat as he advanced towards me. I crawled backwards. Stumbling to my feet, I saw his fist coming and ducked. I hit him on his neck, sending him flailing backwards, eyes wide. His joking smile became a snarl.

Stepping towards me, I turned and ran but hands caught me around the waist and threw me to the floor. I groaned as he sat on top of me, his hands wrapping around my throat. Desperately, I twisted and writhed but he did not let go. Putting my legs around his stomach I summoned all of my strength and switched our position. Leaning backwards, I hit his face with my heel.

Scrabbling to my feet, I fled. Something that attracted the suns light sat near the corner. Without thinking, I hurried to it. It was a shard of tinted glass, missing from the window above it. I wasn't a killer. I didn't think I had the guts but he was charging at me. I had the upper hand, the weapon he hadn't seen.

He stood in front of me, and I stabbed. I didn't know where I had cut and severed him, as I wasn't thinking but when he stumbled away from me, screaming, he was cradling his stump of an arm. In my hand the piece of glass pierced my own skin, making my palm erupt in flames.

Leonardo was stumbling away from me, I went to throw the shard at him but before I could, a gun went off outside. I didn't know who had been shot. Was it Bianca? Or Axel or Josh? I had no way of knowing. My second hesitation was all Marvella needed, he turned and took off. I, realising what had happened, chased after him, cursing at him and shouting. He ran, not away, but to the shots. Following him, I screamed, "Coward!"

If only I had known. If only I was aware of what was to follow.

We had reached the village square. There, a body lay huddled on the floor. I couldn't see who it was. Leonardo stopped to look back at me. "You really are stupid." Men, all dressed in black stepped out from the shadows to surround me. Two men came to stand next to Marvella, one had a girl draped over one shoulder, the other a boy held up by his hair.

"Bianca! Axel!" I screamed. Though unconscious, they were unharmed.

"Letty Lane, daughter of Melony and Joseph, sister to Roy. All three killed by my hand. It is always better to get rid of the lot. Really, I am trying to help you, your grief must be..." He paused, grinning as he cocked his head to one side, "unbearable."

One of his men stepped forward and wrapped his arm in a cloth. I realised that the man unlike the others did not wear black but a robe of brown and green and he was crippled. His skin lay loose on his bones. John Parker. He avoided my eyes, he kept them downcast, away from everyone staring at him.

"What is your plan now, Letty Lane?" he snickered. I watched as he clicked his fingers and two men grabbed my arms pulling me forward. Pushing down on my shoulders, they made me kneel in front of him. I swore at him. Some of his men gasped, others watched nervously on. I still held the glass in my hand, by now it had left its mark in my flesh.

I could tell you I was brave and courageous, that I wasn't scared, that I was fearless, but that would be a terrible lie. My hand was numb, my mind screaming and the men jeering and cheering and the world was falling into itself. Chaos ruled with a golden fist, people like me trembling at its feet.

This was my last chance; my last chance to be a hero. To be, not mine, but everyone else's knight in shining armour. He looked down at me, his face lined with linen, his one hand holding onto a knife rising into the air, to strike the final blow.

The glass, my last resort, sat in my hand and I glared at him, my own heart a roaring lion. Leonardo Marvella shrieked as he brought down his weapon, I too leapt forward, crying for mercy in the heavens.

Hands hit me on the head and I dropped the shard of glass! Digging his knife into my shoulder blade, Marvella cursed. That wasn't his target. The shove had moved me from his direct blow to my heart. I heard crying now, pitiful wails and sobs.

Bianca lay awake on the man's shoulder watching me with eyes large and body limp. "Bianca." She looked at me and cried even harder. "Don't cry, please stop crying, everything is going to be ok." I was not only trying to reassure her but myself for the plan had gone wrong. So horribly wrong!

Hope at its Lowest

I didn't see as someone stepped from the crowd, didn't notice as a boy's voice spoke to Leonardo, "I'll fight you." It was Josh. Gazing upwards from my place on the floor, I groaned, "No! Don't!" He ignored me.

Looking to where the figure had been lying on the floor, I realised that it was gone. A blue wispy boy stood in the shadow of the corner of the square. He caught me looking and winked. Marvella had laughed when Josh had challenged him, but he had accepted, he had ordered his men to leave him and to stand down.

They had backed away, all moving towards the walls. No one bothered to move me. I lay in the middle of the fighting ground. A fever had me in its clutches now and I felt sweat trickling down my forehead.

Josh had been the first one to punch. Leonardo had blocked it with his only hand. I struggled against the pain, writhing, and screaming on the floor. Grunting, I focused my eyes on Bianca, who was on her feet now. Axel stood next to her; both were staring at me.

A cry made me look to the fight, to see Josh lying on the floor, his chest red with the blood that dripped from Marvella's arm. Josh was clinging to his throat as he gasped for air. My hands fumbled and I stifled a yell as something cut my fingers. It was the glass. Taking it in my hand, I crawled towards Leonardo.

I cut his ankle, bringing the glass across the bare flesh hard and deep. A hand took a fistful of my hair and lifted me up by it. I screamed and hit him, clawing wildly. "I have had quite enough of you!" Something cold was traced along my neck making me freeze.

"Letty!" Bianca had started shrieking again and I turned slowly, tears in my eyes to face her. She looked hysterical and Axel was trying to shush her frantically. My shoulder screamed as I tried to free myself. "Help..." I whispered, "Oh, God, please help..." I moaned as he pushed down, irritating the wound.

I saw the shadow of a figure rising behind me, I saw Axel break free from the crowd to sprint towards me, I saw Bianca fight off a man that was holding her arm. Thrusting the glass into his stomach, I twisted it. There was a scream and then blood dripped from my neck, and I gurgled as the liquid dripped from my mouth. I fell forward, hands caught me and cradled me as I writhed.

"Letty!" Axel's face swam in front of me, and I felt as a blackness crawled in around my view. Is that what it felt like to die? The world slowly edging away? I knew people thought death was something to be fearful of but to me it felt peaceful. It was the end of a very, very long day.

I supposed that was the end, the last page turned in the book. However, someone was lifting me upwards and walking away with me in their arms. "What?" I muttered. My eyelids were growing heavier by the second until I could not help but to close them. "It is alright. Sleep." Someone told me.

Drifting off, I smelt burning then heard the cries as hands took my own. They were smaller than the ones who held me and softer as they stroked my cheek.

Book 2

Darkness

I opened my eyes, to a dark room. It was blacked out by wooden planks nailed against the windows and I knew I was alone. "Hello?" I whispered. A face illuminated by a flame, peeked out from behind a door. The person had golden tresses and blood was smeared across one cheek. When she entered, I could see her more closely. I noticed rips in her dress and a cut on the side of her forehead.

"You're awake." She smiled sitting down next to me on the bed. Shouting reached my ears and soon two shadows stood in the doorway. One was attempting to slap the other's face. Setting down the candle next to me on the bedside table, Bianca hurried to them and chided them briskly, "Whatever is the matter with you two? Have we all not agreed that no one here was responsible for the poison? Now, be quiet! You can stay if you stop fussing or else go away and fight each other elsewhere." Though they were both stronger than her and taller, they bowed their heads. "Do you understand?"

"Yes Bianca," They answered.

"Good, I should think so!" She returned to my side and asked, "Does it hurt? I managed to stop the bleeding, but I don't know how long it will take to heal." She motioned to my shoulder. I nodded – it did hurt but it wasn't a sharp fiery pain like it was when it had been first stabbed. I could only really feel it when I moved or put pressure on it.

"You are extremely lucky, he cut some of your neck, but it is barely deep and only cut some of the skin and a bit of flesh."

The boys had decided to go elsewhere, leaving the door open. "What happened? I don't remember much. What did his men do?" Bianca sighed, straightened up and told me, eyes sparkling, "Well, I don't really know what his men did. They just kind of stood there, waiting for their master to rise and shout, 'seize them'."

Bianca squeezed my hand and carried on, "He is dead. Stabbing his stomach was excellent, you had cut it so deep! He bled out. The old sod, the one that looked like he was dead on his feet, burnt his body." Numbly I nodded my head.

"What now?" I asked.

"Now? You rest silly, you can hardly walk north." She scoffed, not unkindly.

"Why walk? We can find horses and ride those."

Bianca eyed me warily and sighed, "It makes me sad; you know sweetheart. I think you have forgotten how to relax. No one is going to hurt you, you are safe."

"And if I am not?"

"I shall kill every single threat to you with my bare hands," Bianca told me ferociously, a glint in her eyes. The tension in my body wavered slightly as she leant forward and stroked my hair. I knew she was the same age as me and that I barely knew her but she was like the mother I never had.

Over the next couple of days, I felt like I was slowly healing. Bianca told me, the day before our departure, that my cheeks had recovered some of their colour, and my eyes had some sparkle in them. My shoulder was less bothersome and the cut in my neck had started to close up. It was going to leave a scar.

Coming back from her visit to the town, Bianca opened the door and set down clothes on the end of the bed. I was standing next to it, finally strong enough to walk. She called Axel and Josh into the room and then told me, "The boys found some horses. They think they belong to the men; they are beautiful, one is a splendid chestnut brown with white patches all over. The other one is as white as snow with a darling black nose. They are strong and well fed, they will be fine creatures to ride."

"There are only two though. Who knows how to ride a horse?" Axel asked, looking at each of us in turn. "I can." I answered.

"So can I," Bianca said.

"Ok, I'll ride with Letty. Josh can ride with Bianca." Axel informed us, ignoring Josh's glare. "I think I would rather ...." Josh began. He cried out as someone thumped him on the back of the head.

"Shut up and just deal with it, Mr Prince." Bianca advised, "Letty doesn't need you to protect her, and from what? Axel? If he wanted to hurt her, he would have done it already!" He grunted. Rolling her eyes, Bianca picked through the clothes throwing some pieces at me.

"They probably don't know what to do now that their master is dead but we cannot risk them recognizing us — they might shoot." Bianca explained. She passed us each a small pile of clothes and sent us to change. The boys went to the other room, leaving me and Bianca alone.

"You alright, sweet?" She asked.

"Yes." I laid my clothes on the bed, "A dress? They're so annoying to ride in."

"I know but women in the North don't wear men clothes and we don't want to attract attention to ourselves." From all the dresses

I had worn in my past, the dress in front of me was most definitely not the most flattering. I slipped it on and went around to tighten the dresses lacings. When the bodice was snug against my figure, I turned to Bianca.

She was struggling to put on the dress. "Not used to such a dress?" I asked, helping her get into it then turning her around to tighten it. She grimaced, "No, I normally just wear slip on one's. The dress she donned was a simple one, pink and floor length. I braided her a crown, leaving half of it tumbling down her back. Handing her a red-moon-coloured cloak, I quickly did my own hair in a half up half down French braid and picked up my own cloak.

Mine was an iris-coloured purple, that covered my blue dress. Together we walked out of the dark room and out into the room next door. Axel was impatiently leaning against the door leading to what I could only presume was outside. He wore trousers, black and a matching jacket with a collar on top of his white shirt.

He did look smart and he seemed to think so too as he winked at me and smugly strutted to the door. "Aren't you forgetting something, Axel?" Bianca asked. Standing still he thought for a moment, walked over to her and kissed her on the cheek. She sighed exasperated, picked up a lonely, isolated green cloak from the floor and draped it over his shoulders for him. Smirking, she pulled the hood, that was three times the size as it needed to be, over his face.

"That is so much better," She commented, then turned to Josh. "Are you ready?" He was. He too wore the clothes that Axel wore but his was brown and he wore a waistcoat. Josh's cloak was a golden colour, like the sun on a fine summer's day. Together we exited the dark room. Squinting, I realised that I had not seen the sun for a day. It was so bright that it blinded me.

I lifted the hood as it gave me shade from the suns piercing gaze. Winter still thrummed in the air, but it had died down a bit leaving only small patches of ice and frost on the houses. Saddled and bridled, the horses were waiting for us behind the house in which we had spent the last few days.

I struggled on how to get onto the horse without riding up my dress to my hips. "Here, let me help." Axel, putting his hands on my waist, lifted me up and put me on the horse's back.

"Thank you." I responded, re-arranging the bothersome skirts around my legs. Handing me the reins, he sat behind me. Bianca and Josh were beside us, their own horse whickering. "You better hold on," I put his arms around my waist and instructed him to not let go.

Digging my heals into the stallion's side he began to trot forward. Bianca rode behind me, keeping a big enough distance that my horse did not kick hers. The further we got from the village the more tense I became. This all seemed too easy.

I looked around but all I saw was the field around me and trees at the edges of the wide stretch of grass. "Letty." Bianca called my name; she steered her horse with some difficulty next to mine. I knew why. Her horse was snorting, its nostrils flaring, and it shook its head. Its ears were pinned down.

My stallion however kept on trotting, watching the ground. "Something is scaring her," I told Bianca. We stopped now, listening intently. "Why isn't yours scared? She looks normal, not like mine," Bianca motioned to her horse, who was breathing heavily and gently pawing the ground.

"It's a he." I said, "My horse is a he." I shook my head, "I don't know. Maybe he is just a brave horse? Or yours is a wimp. He might have scared himself by treading on twig that snapped or something." But I knew it wasn't. Eyes were pressing in all around us but I couldn't see them, rather I sensed them.

"We should go!" Axel said.

"We can't. We don't know whether we are going towards it or away." I told him. Josh looked at me and asked, "What is it, exactly?"

I shrugged, "How am I supposed to know?" My stallion began to move agitatedly, moving forward and backwards. I swore to myself, I said out loud a plan in German. Sighing, I paused, cursed and that time talked to myself in Spanish.

"Whoa!" Axel muttered under his breath.

"We should move but I don't know where!" I told them. "Calm down boy," I leaned forward to stroke the stallion's neck. He nickered, "I know, I know, but you need to ride as fast as you can now."

Sitting up, I looked around me and asked, "Why do you stare?" All three of them grew flustered and averted their eyes away. We couldn't go back to the village - Leonardo's men were too unpredictable. Axel, Bianca, and Josh waited for my answer, but I didn't know what to say.

"Look there they are!" I whipped around, swore, and dug my heels into the stallion's side, urging him to gallop. Scores of men and women were running towards us, each of them holding fire! The thump of the hooves on the ground matched my drumming heart. Bullets flew over our heads; but thankfully, the shrieking became quieter the longer we rode.

Deafening wails

"How many days till we reach the North, Bianca?" I asked that afternoon. The horses were slowing down, tiring from the long ride. "Perhaps a day or two. I cannot be sure though." She had answered, lowering her hood.

"B? How do we know we are going in the right direction?" Josh had questioned. Quickly he added, "Not that I doubt your skills, of course."

Bianca laughed, then informed him, "If the sun's rising at dawn and you face the sunrise, north is to your left. At noon, if you turn towards the sun, north is directly behind you."

No one argued with her.

"We better stop to give the horses some rest."

When the moon was just in sight behind a hill, we all settled down by a fire, a tree looming over us. By now we were peckish, but we had no food on us.

"It is too dark to go hunting now, but me and Bianca will go and catch us some food tomorrow morning," Josh told our rumbling stomach's. We could do nothing but curl up by the fire and try to sleep.

The cloaks kept us warm; no one was in danger of falling asleep and not waking up. That thought made my mind wander to where I had tried so desperately to avoid Harriet. She had been a young, sweet girl, who had a rocky start to life. Her brother had been taken and she was given false hope and died.

False hope I had given. And Dorothy, she had not deserved what happened to her, though in truth, I didn't know if she had lived or died like her sister. I slept dreamlessly that night and awoke to the sun on my face.

Yawning, I sat up. Josh and Bianca had gone, and Axel was still asleep on the other side of the fire. The horses, whose reins had been tied to a tree, lay dozing. Sleepily, I pulled myself to my feet and walked to them, sitting down in front of the one I had rode. "You are handsome," I told him, reaching my hand out to stroke his muzzle. "You're not the first horse I have had to ride away from danger on. There was a darling black horse, when all of this began. We gave him and the other horse to a stable. The chap seemed nice there."

We. Me and Roy.

Smiling sadly, I patted the other horse on the side before saying to them, "Horses are better than people. Horses you can trust. They aren't going to kill you because of money or greed. Humans are like that, so selfishly cruel to each other." I laughed softly at myself – I was talking to horses. They didn't understand a word that left my mouth.

"You are daft," a grumpy voice made me jump. I turned to see Axel up on his elbows watching me with a smile on his lips. His hair was messy, his eyes dopey from sleep. He looked kind of cute. "Morning," I smiled.

"Morning." He grunted in return. A puff of air, blowing my hair, made me turn to the horse that nickered and blew in my face. I fondly patted his nose. "Do you have a name?" I asked it. "How about Nieve?"

Behind me Axel scoffed, "Neive? What kind of name is that?"

"Its Spanish for snow." I told him. He looked oddly at me for a second than shook his head and lay back down. "What? You don't like it?"

"No. No. It's an alright name."

"An alright name?" I swore at him.

"Oi! Watch your mouth!" He was smiling at me, eyes twinkling. The crunch of feet made us both look up to see Bianca and Josh in front of us. Speared by a twig that had been sharpened, a deer sat in both of their arms.

"We are going to eat deer?" I was revolted by the very thought. Its eyes were staring at me glumly. "You can starve if you like." Axel told me, jumping up to help lay the poor creature down.

"Don't be so unkind Axel," Bianca chided, "It was the only creature we saw I am afraid. It tastes alright. Better to eat it than not." I nodded.

"Why don't you go and walk the horses around a bit whilst you wait. You can stretch your legs? They will have to have grass – we have nothing to give them." Bianca suggested. Axel stood and stretched. "I'll go too." He went to untie the knot on the reins.

I undid the one keeping Neive by the tree and looked to Axel. He was swearing under his breath, fiddling uselessly. "Here." Walking around to him, I handed him the reins and coaxed his horse to stand.

We strolled into a field, holding our horses' reins. "Who taught you to ride like you did last night?" He asked stopping so his horse might sniff the ground, hopeful for food.

"My father did. He was fond of horses. My mother not so much," I smiled at the memories that came to me. My hometown had been a cramped place, houses stacked on top of each other and pathways in-between them so narrow you had to walk sideways down them. But around it had been beautiful. Lands of fields and moors, where horses grazed and nature thrived.

Even so, I had mostly been in the town, never seeing the world and now I wanted nothing more than to stay in a safe place for the rest of my life. How times seemed to have changed. Neive munched lazily on clumps of grass.

"Mine's a bit pathetic, isn't he? How come you get the brave horse that doesn't care if death beckons at him?" He asked, watching the horse he held with disgust. I grinned at him and told him, "If your horse didn't fear death too, we would have been burnt alive by those men."

He goggled at me, "You're sticking up for her?"

"I am just saying being scared isn't always a bad thing," I said defensively. Axel scoffed and muttered something under his breath. I just rolled my eyes and asked him, "You ready to go back?" He nodded and together we persuaded his horse and mine to go back to Bianca and Josh.

We saw Bianca, shouting, her hands curled in tight fists. She was screaming at Josh who was looking equally vexed. Her cheeks were flushed red, and she seemed so angry that she was shrieking without real reason.

"Bianca?" She turned on me lava like tears falling down her cheeks. I gave Nieve to Axel then walked to her. "What did he do?" Bianca was going to answer but then looked over my shoulder at Josh and shook her head.

I glanced backwards and saw Josh glaring at her warningly. Something was not right. "Mate?" Axel said. Josh snarled at him. No one spoke for a long while.

Grabbing Bianca gently by the shoulders, I drew her down to sit on the floor next to me. "Let's just eat." The meat was tender and not unpleasant.

We rode swift and serene; it must have been hours since we had begun to ride, when, over trees of lifeless branches, we saw a stone wall. My heart quickened and I bent lower over to whisper into Nieve's ear. How he snorted, his head bucking with his annoyance of the extreme slow pace we have been forced to take. We were riding ever so slowly because, though it was day, nights help had come. The trees offered more darkness than was wise to ride in, for the horses may have fallen, or injured themselves.

The tension in the air seemed to enclose my insides and squeeze them tight in a grip I was unable to shake off. Axel's arms were wrapped against my waist, and I felt his chest leaning against my back, his breath blowing on my neck, my hood down so I could see better. A gate of iron bars glowered down upon us, its ugly demeanour making me shiver.

No man stood in front to welcome us. "Josh..." Axel breathed behind me. Josh had slipped off the other horses back and was walking towards the bars. Cautiously, he pushed it and took a step back as it creaked open. Together, we all gasped as one. This was too queer.

He went to Bianca's horse taking its reins from its rider's hands and guided it through the gate. I followed. No one graced the streets with idle chatter or hot worded mouths. We made our way to a palace, sitting proudly on a throne of a hill.

Josh went to the great oak doors and rapped it calling out, "Hello? Is anyone here?" He was answered by the doors opening and a girl standing before us. She was perhaps older than us, fair with cheeks peppered with freckles, she had a slim nose and a graceful figure, slender and slim. She wore a gown of white velvet, and her hair was twisted in tight curls down her back.

"Sister," the girl's eyes gleamed as she hugged Bianca who returned her embrace. "I hope the travel was not strenuous on you, dear sister? When I saw the weather, how I was frightened for you, but you are here and safe and home, come, a bedroom has already been made for you." With a delicate swish of her hand, she had pirouetted and disappeared inside the palace.

Bianca, taking my hand, laughed and pulled me after her. Inside was a grand place of stone and gold, carpet, and frosted windows. "Now, Josh, I presume," she curtseyed at Josh and asked, "Your surname?"

"Josh Carlten, ..."

"Lady Rebecca, it is honour to finally meet you, Lord Carlten."

"Oh no, I am no Lord," Josh spluttered.

Lady Rebecca smiled, "here you shall be known as one. And you shall be Axel?" Axel nodded briefly and before she could ask him the same question, he responded, "Darlington." Turning to me Lady Rebecca told me, "She never wrote to me about you I am afraid."

"Letty, Letty Lane."

"Ah, you mean Violette?" I nodded. She looked shocked for a second and then a warm expression took hold of her features and she escorted us each to our chambers and instructed us, "Now listen, you must not leave your rooms. When tomorrow comes, you shall eat your breakfast and wear the clothes waiting for you on the sofa. I shall be attending to my Lady, as I do every morning and then I hope we shall catch up soon."

I didn't really think anything of it, I thought they were just very protective of the palace and didn't want complete strangers wandering around. If only I had listened to my inner sense!

Sleep came so profoundly quickly that night, that it had me in its clutches as soon as my head hit the pillow. My sleep would be disturbed though, more than once that night. The first time it was just past midnight. I had slept for only 3 hours, and it was to the most terrible noise.

A wailing cry beseeched my room with its tantalising shrieks. Looking around my room, I saw nothing out of place — everything was where I had left it. My iris-coloured cloak was draped where I had placed it — on the sofa in front of the bed. My dress, that I had not bothered to pick up from the floor when I had changed to my night-gown, still lay strewn on the carpet in front of the hearth.

The shrieks continued but seemed to double in volume and I gasped. It was a child's screams, one of a baby, but it was not the natural cry of a new-born, but of terror. I curled myself up on the bed to try and block it out but the fear in it was making me quiver. What was happening to that poor child to force him to cry out in so much suffering?

I covered my ears with my pillow and tried to talk to myself out of it. My tongue, that was forming words, was muttering Spanish; like it was trying to cast a spell. "It's not real," I told myself, "This is all just a nightmare! I shall wake up and this will all just be a dream." "Oh, sleep please take me," I prayed. And a miracle happened - it did.

The second time it awoke me, I was not so surprised, and sleep had such a powerful grip on me, I thought it was just the mere wind. I could not go back to sleep for hours though, and by the time I had drifted off again, I had come back to my senses and my own trepidation had returned. It had begun to haunt me in my dreams as well.

Yet again that night, I was aroused by the sound of that child. It was fainter now and slowly dying away, knowing sleep was not going to come again, I slipped out of bed and sluggishly walked to the door. When I tried to open it, it was stuck fast! Frantically, I twisted it. It would not open!

I gazed around the room until my eyes locked upon glass doors, that were covered by white curtains and lead to a balcony. Running, I tried to open them and to my great relief they swung open. Walking out, I opened my mouth in surprise. A light, in the distance, twinkled at me. It was memorising beautiful.

"Letty?" I jumped at the sight of Bianca. She too had a Balcony that was next to mine. She was leaning against the railings, her eyes too looked as though she had been staring at the strange brightness.

"Did you hear it too, the wailing?" She asked, shivering.

I asked, "The wailing of a child?" though I knew that was what she was talking about. Bianca nodded, "It was horrible, they locked my doors as well."

"Same here." I leaned on the railings as well and looked out at the light. Two figures were dancing in the front of the light, one was a girl, with a dress twirling around her, the other a boy his hands on her waist.

"Hello." A face peered out of a window.

"Hi Axel."

"Strange night for you ladies as well then?" Me and Bianca nodded. He joined us in our gazing at the people and commented, "They look like angels with the light all around them."

Stir in the plot

"Lady Violetta?" I turned to see a maid standing in the doorway, keys in her hands.

"I will see you two later." I bid the others morning and then left. The maid had set a gown on my bed and was ushering me into it. It was a splendid gown, purple laced and flattering. She smiled at me, "You have lovely eyes Miss, so bright and full of happiness. A few people here have such blue eyes as you."

She smoothed out my hair, that was left flowing silkily down my back, it reached my waist and shone in the sunlight beautifully. Tying a golden necklace around my neck, she told me, "Now, My Lady, Lady Rebecca is busy, but you are welcome to walk around. Some rooms are locked so you mustn't even try to get into those. Should I bring your breakfast to you, or do you prefer to dine downstairs?"

"Here is fine... what's your name?"

"Suzanne, My Lady."

"That will be all Suzanne." She curtseyed and left. I felt a pair of eyes on me and a smile blossomed on my lips as I knew who it was. "Mami?" A delighted laugh filled my chamber and sure enough, my Mami, in her petal dress stepped out from the shadows at the corner of my room.

"Hello, my darling girl," She beamed, "I knew you could do it my love. You thought you could not do it, but how you had looked that monster in the eye for the last time!"

I felt the corners of my mouth lift. "He is proud of you, Letty. Roy is so proud." Nodding numbly, I was aware of a singular tear falling down my cheek. "Your Papi has a message for you, one you must take care of," I cocked my head to one side. "You are the best thing that could happen to this Kingdom. You shall be history."

She strolled towards me and stroked my cheek, "You will need that knowledge for what is to come, darling Letty. You are a clever girl and I know you shall know when the right time is to leave this world behind." Mami reached forward and kissed me on my brow, "Goodbye for now, little seed."

Floating to the door, she flew away.

"My Lady?" I looked towards the door.

"You can come in," Suzanne entered, a tray in hand. "Thank you, Suzanne. Oh, what was that noise last night, the crying?"

"Twas nothing but the wind, it often sounds like a child crying," I frowned at her. "That is what they all say, my lady, it always has sounded like that, well ever since Lady Amelie came to live here with her baby."

"Who?"

"The King's sister, My Lady."

"Ah, I see."

I sat down on the sofa in front of the hearth and asked, "Suzanne couldn't you shut the door and make a fire, its chilly in here?" She bobbed her head and hurried to work. I asked her, "What is there to do here?"

"There is a library, grandest in the kingdom. Walks around the garden grounds are always lovely and there is a music room and of course the town is splendid as well." A flame grew bigger, the more she fed it wood and she stood up from the position she had sat in to tend to the fire.

A table sat before me, circular and delicate looking. Suzanne placed a teacup and teapot in front of me and filled the cup with hot tea, "Sugar?"

"No, thank you, that's fine." She placed a bun in front of me and cut it in half, delicately spreading jam in the centre. A knock at the door summoned Suzanne to it and she opened it.

She closed it slightly and informed me, "It is Lord Darlington. Shall I invite him in?" I waved my hand and Suzanne let Axel in.

"Hello." I smiled. He wore a suit, green with a white shirt. He came and sat next to me on the settee. "Bianca said she is going to see Rebecca. I came across Josh on my way here. He was sweating and hurrying back to his room."

"That is strange."

"What do you plan to do then today?"

"Go to the gardens maybe. You are welcome to join."

He nodded, "I shall." Suzanne set a cup of tea next to him as well as a roll, and together we ate with odd idle chatter.

Here, winter seemed to not exist, it was not freezing but just chilly. We stepped out into the air, and I closed my eyes. A breeze blew against my face.

"It's beautiful..." I said, and indeed it was. Nature thrived, and how the sweet smell of petals and the fresh air, lingered on my tongue. Oh how the combination of the birds chirping and the trees swaying, sent me lullingly into a calm trance. Together, me and Axel strolled forward, walking on the pebbled path.

"It is so very peculiar here," I commented, looking up to see the branches of trees, hanging over us like umbrellas to protect us from the sun. If you were to fall from the sky, they would catch you like nets, their hands cupped, so you might not carry on falling.

"Peculiar? What is so peculiar about it?" Axel asked, a scowl settling on his brow.

"You needn't look so glum, you know. My Grandpa Eddie used to say, 'if you scowl long enough each day then the lines upon your forehead shall stay forever!'" Until that very moment I had forgotten all about Grandpa Eddie and I found myself wondering how he was.

"Pff," Axel chuckled, shaking his head. I felt his eyes on me and then heard as he said, "You have gone quiet, what are you thinking about?"

"Oh, it is nothing. It is just……" I paused, "Well, Grandpa Eddie has no-one right now. Mami and Papi are dead, so he doesn't have them and me and Roy are not there, and all his friends think he is mad."

"And is he?" he asked quietly as if it were not a question, he should like the trees to hear, "Is he mad?"

"Oh, in the very least!" I exclaimed, "If he was any madder, he would be sent off to an asylum and die there, but he is not quite that bad, just isn't really that good in the head most days."

Axel nodded solemnly and I asked, "What about you? Where is your family?" He stopped walking for a moment, looking down at his feet. "You do not have to tell me, Axel. It was a simple question powered by curiosity, nothing more."

"No…. I….. I shall like to tell you." I stood patiently watching as he shuffled nervously, clicking his tongue as if that would help the words come out. The stern oaks seemed to be waiting as well, they did not stir but like me were holding their breath in anticipation.

"I have a little sister, Margaret, she is five. She loves flowers. She used to sit by them on the fields next to our village and talk to them like they were her friends. She used to tell me, if I had to choose one group of people on this planet to be my best friends forever it would be my dear lilies', for they are beautiful and enchanting. They sit around all day and they listen so nicely, they laugh and cry in all the right places and they are simply my best friends."

I smiled at this. "She used to wear them in her hair, she said the yellow lilies looked splendid against her black waves." We started to walk again, closer this time. Together, me and the trees breathed. "And my mother, why she was wise, she was a herbalist. She used to get Margaret and me to go and pick them when we were not at school and give them to her."

"So, why did you leave?"

"War." He told me, "My father had been sent to war years ago. He had lived so long but then died just weeks before I had to leave. They were going to take me as well. I was not a soldier. I had never fought. So, I had to run away. I met Bianca and Josh in the beginning of their journey north and joined them."

"I am so sorry, Axel that sounds horrible," I linked my hand with his. He looked surprised for a second then squeezed my hand in return. It felt strange to walk hand in hand with a boy - I had never thought I would.

For a split second, I thought I saw a blue wispy figure in the form of a boy, watching me from behind a tree. He had waved and smiled and with a flick of his hand sent a gust of wind blowing my hair.

"Axel, do you believe in ghosts?" He looked at me for a second and then informed me, eyebrows raised, "Well, if you can convince me they are real, then I might start to believe."

"What a good answer!" Swaggering towards us, Roy laughed. "Do not look so scared my friend! I am Roy Lane, at your service," he mocked bowed and then straightened up again.

I keenly said, "Roy, must you be such a nuisance? Be nice!" That sent him into a fit of laughter and then he jumped forward and captured me in his embrace, "What words fall from that bewitching tongue of yours, dear sister! Oh, but we both know, its a witch's tongue!"

I raised my fist at him and cursed at him in German, calling him such names that delicate ears, such as ones belonging to ladies and children, should not hear. "Letty, how dare you talk to me like that!" Roy, scolded, jokily. I rolled my eyes and put up my middle finger at him. "There it is!" He hooted, releasing me and dancing backwards singing to himself, "There she goes, Letty Lane, try to scold her in vain. Letty Lane, Letty Lane, try to scold her in vain!"

Then something strange happened. An angry expression took hold of Roy, as he saw something behind us. Sticking out his tongue, he vanished. "There you guys are!" Josh was strolling towards us. Quickly, I let go of Axel's hand.

"Hello, Josh," I said, "How are you today?"

"Fine, who were you talking to just now? It was a boy's voice and certainly not Axel's," He was looking at us slyly which made me shift uncomfortably. Perhaps, Axel sensed my discomfort for quickly he retorted, "It was no one, you must have been hearing things!"

"Indeed?"

"Yes of course, Josh, we both heard nothing," I backed Axel up. Josh inclined his head and then told me, "Letty, may I ask you something?"

"Go ahead."

"Say, love could bring you the peace you need but to have it would be to betray someone. Would you be with the most beautiful women you have ever seen and get rid of someone, or cast that memorising lady out of your life and be close to someone else?"

"Well, dear Josh, that is no simple question!" I exclaimed. "Love is many things, but it is not a game. You cannot cheat it and to simply throw it aside, is to leave something unfinished and leave a part of you behind."

Josh was staring at me so intently as if each word I spoke needed to be remembered exactly. "But that also depends on who that person you are to betray for love is and how deep your bond is severed!"

"Deeper than anything you can sow back together!" Josh huffed, going slightly pale. The trees loomed closer in, and perhaps if they were real, they would have nudged each other out of the way to get a better view of us. "Dear Josh, who is the lover? And who is to be betrayed?"

"Nobody worth mentioning, it was just something I found myself curious over!" Josh told us, curtly. He bowed briskly at us and then hurried off disappearing behind the nosey oaks.

"That was... odd," I said, scrunching up my nose. Axel agreed and then together we continued our strolling, our hands brushing against each other as we walk, but never for long.

Save yourself

That afternoon, when the sun had tired and was lowering down for sleep, Bianca and Lady Rebecca came to my quarters where Axel was sitting on the sofa. "Good afternoon, my dear, I hope the day has enticed you in its many wonders?"

"As much as one needs to be entertained my Lady," I replied, standing up so she might sit down. She lowered herself gracefully onto the sofa, sitting at the edge and fanning herself with the green fan she held in her hands.

Bianca stayed standing, her hair a bleached yellow, from the sun's dim light peeking through the curtains. "Letty?" Bianca began a frown forming on her features, "Have you seen Josh today?"

Before I could answer, Lady Rebecca cut in, "I am sure he has just been wandering over the palace's grounds, or gone for a walk. It is the best time to go for one. The sun is just in the right position, over the trees!"

The evening went by tiringly slow and by the end of it, conversations were held sluggishly and words were slurring together. Lady Rebecca left hours before any of us went to bed, apparently, she was going to check on her lady, but she never returned. Suzanne came to us and whispered, "Axel, might you come with me?"

Axel, though brows furrowed together, bade us goodnight, and followed Suzanne, leaving a plausible distance between him and her.

"That was unnerving, I must say," Bianca whispered, watching the door with hope glittering in her eyes. "B?"

"Hm?"

"This place, the people, something's just not right,"

Bianca gazed at me and biting her bottom lip told me, "Well, all palaces have their secrets, I suppose, and we have only been here a day and a night. We better just keep our heads down and get on with it and hopefully some things will come into the light."

She spoke so earnestly, and with such a strong voice, I dare not question her. The look she bestowed upon me was one of clear defiance. "It is quite late, Bianca, you better head to bed," I said amidst the silence, "Come."

Bianca, with grace and one of tired softness, padded to the door. I tuck my knees up to my chest and held a cup of tea in my hands staring into the flickering beasts of the flames. "Letty?" My name was called, sleepily. I turned, to see Bianca, hand poised on the door handle. "It is locked."

"Locked?"

"Yes, locked."

Pinching my temple, I massaged it before saying, "You better stay the night then." Walking back towards me, she plopped herself back onto the sofa, curled-up and closed her eyes.

Walking to my dressing table, I untied the knot on the back of my dress and slipped out of it, pulling my night dress over my head. I lifted the covers on my bed and lay down, the softness of it hugging my body.

We both found no trouble in falling asleep; it was blissfully quite as we fell into a slumber. But what awoke us was more terrible than the child crying. Something was snuffling. I brushed the sleep from my eyes and went up on my elbows to watch the door.

The snuffling noise changed into a grunting noise as if something was finding it hard to breathee. It continued to rise in volume as if it was getting closer. I felt a shiver run down my spine and I could not move, paralyzed with fear.

"Letty?" I jumped, but turned only to see Bianca, perched on the end of the sofa. "Letty?" She wailed.

A scream that wrapped the air with its sheer agony, made Bianca gasp and scurry towards me, diving under the covers.

Scraping along the walls was a claw, it was in the corridor now and Bianca was clinging to me. Both of us staring at the door, tense and afraid to move. Sobbing, Bianca covered her mouth with her hands, as a snout, with wiry hair coming out of it, snuffled under the door. I held my breath as the nose moved up and down, as if trying to smell out its prey.

Bianca clung to me even tighter, putting her head in my shoulder. I could not tear my eyes away from it. It snuffled one more time before retreating and making its way further down the corridor.

A tapping noise made Bianca give out a whimper and I found the source of the noise was coming from the glass doors leading out into the balcony. A boy stood shivering out there. I gently disentangled Bianca from me and ran to the door, cast it open and threw myself into Axel's arms. I heard crying from the bed and saw Bianca tears falling down her cheek the covers up to her nose.

"What was it?" Axel asked shaking me slightly. Words failed me and Bianca was now rocking back and forth agitatedly. He guided me to the fire that was still burning brightly. Dropping me down on the sofa, he went over to Bianca and somehow coaxed her out of the bed. As soon as she had let go of the covers, she fell to her knees. Stooping down, Axel lifted her up in his arms and placed her next to me.

"What happened?" Axel pushed on.

Warmed by the fire, I looked at him and whispered, "A creature, a ghastly creature was there," My gaze drifted to the door, "He was trying to smell something out. Or..." A lump built in my throat, "someone."

The shadow dweller

An age seemed to have passed. Bianca unable to remain still any longer, jumped to her feet and turned to look at us. Axel had sat down in the middle of us, now he gazed with concern at Bianca.
"I don't want to ....."
But whatever she didn't want to do was not heard as she looked up, her mouth open in a scream. Her eyes locked onto something in the corner and she collapse unconscious to the floor.
Axel sprung to his feet, shouting her name. Dread building inside of me, I turned around to see...
A woman lurking in the corner of the room, hiding in the shadows. I felt my eyes widen and watched on as the lady stepped out into the light of the moon. She wore a black gown, with a v neckline that went to her waist, covering only half of her chest. Her eyes bore into mine with red blood like stains dripping down to her stomach. A black substance fell down her cheek from her eyes. Her black hair fell down her back, the ends of them stained with something white. Her nails were like claws, her sleeves dangling and ripped.
She looked at me with venom and hatred and opening her mouth, she screamed. It was an ear-piercing shriek that made me cover my ears as though they might burst from the pain. Looking behind me, I saw Axel too had collapsed to the floor.
A name drifted into my mind and like a curse fell out of my mouth. A blue ghostly figure flew out of my heart and charged like a bull straight at the woman as she gave one last scream and then vanished.

My door flew open and Suzanne, followed by Lady Rebecca and a lady I had not seen before, hurried into the room. Seeing Axel and Bianca unconscious, Lady Rebecca, ordered Suzanne to go and fetch guards and the physician.

"My Lady?" Lady Rebecca asked as the lady I knew nothing of, drifted towards me. She reached out and touched my cheek looking into my eyes, "You saw her, didn't you?" I simply stared at her. She smelled of alcohol, but it was clear to me she was in no way drunk. The lady held herself gracefully. She was much older than everyone here, perhaps in her 50s but she was still very beautiful. Honey blonde hair with white whisps at the front, framed her face which was friendly and gave a sad smile.

"I am sorry Violette," Lady Rebecca turned, "this is her majesty, The Queen. A lady comes to visit her now and then, but no one has ever seen her. As Her Highness is always drunk of late, I and the rest of her subjects have decided she must be imagining things. Drinking does peculiar things to the mind!"

The Queen ignored this comment and watched me carefully. I had the rather strange feeling that's she was sizing me up for something. Then, letting her hand drop from my cheek, stepped back. She let Lady Rebecca guide her out of the room.

Suzanne had returned with the guards and physician. Together they lifted Axel and Bianca on the bed. The physician revived them by dabbing a liquid onto a cloth, holding it against their noses.

"My Lady?" Suzanne asked. I ignored her and stared into the fire, my brain was alight with questions. Why was that child crying? Why is Lady Amelie, the Queen's sister not helping her own child? What has been going on with Josh? And who was that woman, and what has the Queen got to do with her?

Having so many questions and no answers had my mind in knots. A man was crouching in front of me shaking me slightly. "Letty?" I looked at him. It was not the physician as I thought it was but Josh. "Are you alright?"

Slowly, I nodded but a kind of fog was lowering into my mind. I tried to fight it off, but it just kept on getting thicker and thicker. I felt dazed, like the world around me was not there or as if it moved swimmingly and swaying. Josh's face was gone and replaced by what I could only presume was the Physician's. He had me by the elbows and was guiding me to lie down on the sofa.

Before I lost consciousness, I looked towards the fire. Standing in front of it was the lady. She was smiling viscously at me. I saw fangs coated in blood. The last thing I saw before the world was gone, was her face that had resumed its emotionless stare.

The bear, or something else

I felt dizzy as I awoke with the sun on my face and the sense that I was somewhere different from where I had fallen asleep. Sitting up, I noticed I was in my bed; Suzanne was busying herself with building up the fire and the other people that I had fallen asleep in the same room with had gone.

"Oh, mercy me!" Suzanne cried, hurrying to my bedside, "You did have my knickers in a twist! Been crying and moaning all night you have keeping me on my toes!" She blushed at herself and bowing her head added, "Forgive my lame talk, My Lady, sleep does get my tongue all twisted."

I smiled at that and told her, "Sorry to keep you awake. If you like you can help me get ready, then go to bed. I am sure I can keep myself occupied." She threw me a look of deep liking and then bustled on, "How very courteous of you My Lady, I shall do just that!"

With a smile ablaze in her eyes, she left and returned with a gown in a charming green. Helping me into it and fixing my hair in waves, she bid me good day before leaving.

A knock at the door, made me look up later that morning. I was curled up on the sofa, a book on my lap, "It is open!" I called out. Josh came in holding something behind his back. "Hello, dear Josh, what have you got there?"

"A present," He smiled standing in front of me.

"Oh? What is the occasion?" I sat up, placing my book beside me.

He handed it to me and explained, "No occasion just wanted to thank you for good advice yesterday!" My smile faltered slightly but Josh seemed to have not noticed. My hands shaking, I pulled on the ribbon as it fell free from its bow on my lap and then lifted the lid of the box.

"Oh..." I breathed. In the palm of my hand sat a necklace, a sapphire blue.

"I thought it would bring out your eyes," He told me, "I have another present for you, but I am afraid you shall have to wait for tomorrow evening."

A gruff voice came from the door, "Why my dear friend how mysterious you are!" Axel stood leaning against the door frame. He watched Josh with a cold expression, stepped across the room and stood next to me, "Letty, might I show you something?"

I put the necklace on the table and stood up. Looking quite peeved at the interruption, Josh glared at Axel. I was surprised holes did not appear in his chest! "Thank you, Josh, it is beautiful, I shall wear it when I get back."

Taking Axel's arm, I let him guide me out of my chamber and outside. "Axel?"

"What is it?"

"What did Suzanne want with you?"

"She didn't want anything, she just led me to the library and told me someone wanted to talk to me. When they never showed up, I went back to my room and woke up to this snuffling nose. It was clear to me it was alive. When it went past my room, I could hear it had stopped moving. I knew it must have been outside your room. I waited 'till it left, to go and see you but my door was locked. I remembered how close my window was to your balcony and climbed to it and then knocked on your door."

I nodded and then looked around us. We were in the middle of the forest with the curious trees again. "What are we..." The question trailed off as something caught my attention. I ran to it, stroking its bark with my fingers. It had been hurt. Claw marks much like a bear's had been engraved into it.

"Letty, she is back." I spun around. There, the woman in black stood but she was not alone. Another woman, one with claws, black and rotting and a white dress that looked like webs spun around her. Her eyes were black beads, her hair white and floor length, and she was ashen faced. She looked half dead.

"What are you?" I asked, "Who are you?" They did not answer. "What are your names?"

They glared at us, not speaking. The one in white glided away, the black woman, her eyes growing wide, began to scream. Me and Axel both flew our hands to our ears. The woman vanished in a black smoke cloud.

"Axel," I said. He looked at me. "Axel, tonight, you, me, Bianca in the library. We are going to find out what is going on."

A heart full of deep loathing

That night came with a mixture of excitement and fear. When it came, I bid Suzanne goodnight. When I could not hear the clump of her feet, I climbed out of bed, slipped on a gown that was light and long and hurried out. The door was thankfully not locked yet. Axel and Bianca were waiting for me outside my room.

Axel wore a black suit so he might hide in the shadows, Bianca a dark pink gown like the one I wore. Making our way to the library, we walked down the corridor, Bianca in front. Axel grabbed her from the waist, one hand over her mouth to stifle her cry and pulled her to him as a guard walked down the corridor.

As quietly as we could, we tiptoed to the library door and slipped inside. It was a grand room, full of scattered books and ceiling high bookshelves. I had never seen quite so many books in my life! We all stood there, gaping for a long while but grew aware of our vulnerability in the wide open and hurried behind some bookshelves. Books covered us, giving us a shield from unwanted eyes but small gaps between them so we might see what was happening. "Letty!" Bianca hissed, "Letty if we die because of you, I am going to kill you!"

Axel put his hands over her mouth as the door to the library opened and a familiar voice came into the room, "Josh, my Josh, this is betrayal to Bianca," Lady Rebecca said, "but I have to admit I cannot let you go!"

"You don't have to, we can be together I am willing to forget

Bianca, if you love me, you should be too." Bianca's eyes were growing wider and wider, brimming with tears.

"My darling, if it is a matter of love, then I love both of you," Lady Rebecca's voice was soft with tears. "But I do love you more I suppose. God gave me Bianca as a sister, a companion for my younger years. But he gave me you, to keep forever."

Oh, this was bad, very, very bad. Bianca began to struggle against Axel's hold on her. "B!" I whispered, low enough Josh and Lady Rebecca could not hear, "B, listen to me." I grabbed her by the shoulders and forced her to look at me, "B, if you give us away now, we are busted. We shall never find out what is going on."

Bianca stopped struggling and nodded. Axel let go of her. When we turned back, Josh and Lady Rebecca were holding hands as they walked out of the library. Me and Axel cast each other a glance. Crouching down, all three of us waited until we heard something.

We did not have to wait long, no more than an hour had passed, before feet were running along the corridor and the library door was flung open, shrieking cries of a child filling the room. "Oh, my baby, you must hush. He is coming!" A woman held a wailing baby in her arms.

Her fair hair fell into the baby's face as she looked down at its scrunched-up features. "Mama, is here my love, oh my baby please, he is coming, he is coming!" She was sobbing now and glanced at the door as a shadow fell through the gap at the bottom. "Oh God!" She screamed, "Oh God! Mercy! Mercy! Have Mercy on my child, protect it from that monster! Oh God! My God!"

Scraping at the door made her run backwards, the child a wailing banshee. I looked at Bianca and Josh and then back at the scene and saw someone standing in front of the desperate mother. It was the woman in white, her dress a see-through web, her eyes not so beady but full of sympathy.

"He has already taken my baby boy! Not Rhea, I beg you! Not Rhea!"

"Hush! Your child was taken from you a night ago. My sister watched it happen and fled to warn the girl, Bianca."

"Warn, warn that fool of what?" The mother screamed, "My baby boy is dead!" She fell to her knees in her despair and clutched at her blonde locks.

"She is in perilous danger; the monster knows her blood, can smell it, like it could smell your children's."

"What is there to be done, Guinevere? Or is there no hope left for me?"

"The creature outside of this door is like no other, it is the only one of its kind and therefore has no name or purpose. It feeds from blood; it chooses its prey long before it has even met them and comes every night to seek them out."

Guinevere bent low and whimpered, "Might I hold Rhea a moment more? Keep her safe?" The woman seemed fearful and hugged the baby cradled in her arms even closer to her chest. "Amelie," The woman in white said, "Amelie, this child though you might not see it, is this kingdom's future and pride! She must be protected and only I can give her that!"

Looking at her baby with love shinning in her face, the mother bent down to kiss her child's forehead and stood up handing her over to the woman in white. As soon as the baby touched Guinevere's arms it stopped crying, "I shall take the very best care."

"Thank you." The mother bowed her head.

Walking to the window, Guinevere sat on the windowsill and gracefully lowered herself down. The white whisps at the end of her hair the last thing we saw. Another figure stepped out from the shadows, this time, the woman in black. "Why are you here, Omisha?" The mother snapped, turning her back on the woman.

"She is here you know, Amelie, the girl, Bianca." Omisha looked directly in our direction, catching Bianca's eyes in-between the books we were peeking through. Bianca's breathing hitched in uncertainty. Taking her hand, I guided both of us to the other women.

"I appear to have alarmed you the night before this one. I assure you that was not my purpose."

"You screamed at us." Bianca sniffed.

"No, not at you, I am a Banshee, I wail to warn people of death. This case was the Queen's sister's child."

"Oh," Bianca gasped, eyes glittering with unshed tears, "I am sorry, Lady Amelie"

"It was not your fault dear."

The woman in black was staring at me. "What is it? Why do you stare at her?" Bianca asked.

"Oh, my dear child," The woman in black sighed stepping forward, "You have suffered a great deal from death's beautiful work! I can feel it's presence on you! That man. Leonardo Marvella, I saw him die you know, my husband thought I should like to watch him suffer."

"I am sorry," I said blankly. "Beautiful?"

"Yes! You cannot see it of course but from me and my husband's eyes we see their soul drift upwards, specks in the sky. The brighter the particles the greater the loss."

"And who is your husband?" Axel asked.

The woman in black smiled, her fangs showing and answered, "He is Death."

Bianca shifted uncomfortably, caught in the mother's tantalising stare. "Lady Amelie?" I asked.

"Oh," She breathed shakily, "My child, I am sorry! It is just I can see you have no idea what danger you are in!"

Bianca, in panic, looked at me for a second but when I shrugged, she drew her attention back to the conversation.

"A skeleton with a robe?" The woman in black was laughing. "That is what you humans think he looks like?" Bianca looked offended and her cheeks were a dusk pink.

"No, he has a man form, black hair and tattoos all over him. They are alive you know. I think they speak to him for sometimes I think I hear him talking to them when they think I am not listening!"

"And your sister? Is she married?"

"Yes, her husband is Life and her wife Nepheete, a siren."

Before anyone could answer, a screech came from the door that shook as if something was trying to knock it off its hinges. The mother gave a wail of fear and collapsed on the floor. Out of the shadows, yet again, walked a figure. He wore a black cloak and held a scythe in his hands.

The wood of the door was screaming as it was slammed against by the creature. The woman in white, with grace, hurried to the man and put her hands on his shoulders and shook her head. She coaxed one of his hands from the weapon and took it in her own. "Letty Lane." She called.

I turned to look at her. "You are destined for greatness and a future you neither thought for yourself, nor want. But in the end, that is the reason why you shall be the best one there is!"

Omisha and Death turned and went back into the shadows, their black demeaner making them camouflaged as they stepped through the wall and out into the night air. Still the creature ran at the doors making perilous screams of hunger. Axel stooped and lifted Amelie to her feet, and just before the door was thrown open shouted, "Run!"

Books were cast to the floor as we hurtled towards the spiral staircase leading onto the second floor of the library. "Oh God, oh God!" Amelie screamed as the creature became louder and louder as it gained on us.

My ankles twisted with each step. I was pushed upstairs almost falling over the railing as Amelie forcefully made her way to the front. I cussed at her, my tongue twisting in an ugly, angry language.

Soon, we made it to the top of the stairs and with dread, saw the monster climbing the wall like a spider towards us. Breaking into a run, we scarpered to take shelter between bookshelves, covering our heads as volumes fell on top of us, the monster's claws scraping against the wood.

I saw Bianca in front of me fall to the ground shouting incoherently at Amelie whom she had tripped over. Never before had I heard such wild curses from Bianca, she jumped to her feet and ran, her hair and gown flowing behind her. Axel ran past Amelie, the creature sniffing the ground.

I took a handful of the mother's sleeve and dragged her behind me. The creature slowed down now, pacing towards us with malicious pleasure in its hope filled eyes. "Letty!" Bianca was screaming, "Letty, it is a dead end! We are trapped!" And the monster knew it. It revelled in its prey's despair, its laughter sounded as if it was choking and when it sidled past us, claws raised, it did so with ease.

Bianca whimpered as it stopped in front of her, licking its lips with a lizard-like tongue. "B, do not move!" Her bottom lip quivered; saliva dripped from the monster's mouth as it loomed over her. I saw her nails digging into her palm and her legs to give way under her as she collapsed shivering at its feet.

Amelie stood next to me, hands clasped in prayer, muttering to herself. Breathing heavily, sweat dripping down his forehead, leaning against books for support, was Axel. "B." I said slowly, taking small steps towards the creature. Crouching down, keeping my eyes on its back, I picked up a book and with caution stood once again.

Something helped my fear leave me, something pumping through my veins helped me raise that book above my head like it a was a sword and bring it down upon the creatures back. It made a wailing sound and then turned, its tail whipping around, sending Bianca flying. Glowering down at me, I saw its face for the first time. It was almost bald apart from a few clumps of grey hair, its nose was one of a wolf, its body almost human like.

It was naked and its skin was pink and wrinkled like a baby rat's. It was heaving and making dreadful noises. "B," I muttered. "Run." But she was already speeding back down the stairs, Amelie right behind her. Axel was standing up straight now and was looking around with trepidation.

There upon a wall stood a sword, it was rusty and unkempt, and had been hung and abandoned with no pride in the corner, a golden plaque in front of it. A fetid stench made me gag as the creature sniffed; I had a rather uncanny feeling he was smelling my blood. Not knowing whether I was going to be turned into a meal or slaughtered, I clenched my eyes shut. I was begging for it to be fast and painless. I waited and waited but what I thought would be my end never came. A final sniff, then a screech so high pitched I thought my ear drums would break, filled the library.

I screamed and fell to the floor covering my ears in pain. Then, there was a hissing sound and the smash of glass. When I looked up, I let out a wobbly laugh. Blood sat in pools before me and a window further down had been shattered, a monster shaped hole where glass should have been. Someone timidly touched my shoulder. I jumped and would've screamed had I not glanced upwards.

Axel was crouched beside me, "Here," He offered me his hand and together we walked away from the scene of blood and shattered glass.

The Queen and her husband

The next morning, I waited for Suzanne to come wake me, even though I had not slept and was wide awake. When she came in, she greeted me with her usual enthusiasm and bustled around me preparing a bath and making tea, getting me dressed, and moving with so much speed it made me dizzy to watch her.

"So, My Lady, what have you got planned today?" She asked bubbly, combing my hair.

I sighed and caught her eye in the mirror, "Nothing exciting, I have a visit to make." Suzanne nodded wisely as if she knew exactly what had happened last night and why I need to talk to Bianca.

"Well, My Lady, The Queen has asked for your presence this morning in her chamber, so I do hope you did not plan to go and do your visit now?"

"No, that shall be fine, I shall speak with the Queen." I stood.

Suzanne helped me fashion a corset and a structured skirt, black with swirling gold patterns. My hair remained falling down my back, a gentler orange in the sun's light. "I shall go to her now, Suzanne, where is it she wishes to meet?"

"In her chambers, My Lady, I shall show you the way."

Suzanne rapped on the door and stepped aside to let me enter. The freckled face of Lady Rebecca answered. Ushering me in, she stood beside the closed door as I took in the room. For a Queen's chamber, it was simple and dull, paintings hung on the walls, most looked as if they were painted by herself and there was very little furniture.

Her Majesty lay on the couch, a wine glass in her hand, she looked up, her eyes glassy. "Oh! Violette, was it?"

"'Letty' Your Highness."

"Oh yes, Letty. Now, I want to ask you some questions my dear. Answer them truthfully and everything shall be just fine."

I nodded slowly, "Alright."

"Firstly, have you seen the woman in black? Does she haunt you dreams too?"

"Yes, Your Highness."

"Yes?" She asked. "Good, good. Now what do you think about Josh?"

Unable to stop myself I cursed. The Queen went very quiet and then said, "Well, that is explanatory on its own."

"What about Bianca?"

"I have nothing against dear Bianca," I told her, perhaps unwisely because she looked slightly peeved.

"And Axel?"

"He is a kind soul. I have no bad comments about him, Your highness."

"And, Letty, would you say they like power?"

"Who doesn't, Your Majesty?" I answered bitterly. The Queen's face was growing slightly pink but I didn't think it was from anger.

"And have they shown any desire to overthrow their rulers?"

"Well, technically speaking you are not yet their ruler, they are just staying in your palace as visitors and, no, I do not think they would desire something so impossible."

"Impossible?"

"Well, it can't be easy to kill the Queen and King, can it?"

The Queen shared a look with Lady Rebecca, whose face I had not seen throughout this rather unnerving conversation. Before I could turn to look at it, she had already walked out of the room.

"Do you wish for power yourself Letty?"

"Um," I stuttered, "Well, as a daughter of a Lady and Lord I have always been high up in the hierarchy. So, in some sense, I already had all the power I have ever needed."

"So, you admit you would like more power?"

"Well......" I started.

"That shall do!" The Queen barked, taking a slurp of her suspiciously wine looking drink. I was very aware of the time – only 11 in the morning! Feeling I had said things I shouldn't have, I stood, curtseyed, and left, feeling quite empty and confused.

"And that is what happened?" Bianca asked at lunch that afternoon, a frown ruffling her feature. She looked at me with her dazzling smile and told me, "That is strange, but I cannot say I am that surprised."

I raised my eyebrows lifting the cup in my hands to my lips. "Yes well, she did seem shocked when she thought you saw the...." she coughed and looked around, ".....well ...um... the woman in black."

"You do not believe me, do you?" I asked.

"Well, I did see a woman and she was indeed in black, but it could have easily been the shadows and it was only for a second or two! Come on Letty, it is not really the most believable story!"

"That's fine, you think I am mad. That's fine, I do not need you to believe me." I stood, smoothing my dress with the palm of my hand, "Good day to you Bianca." Leaving the door open as I flew down the corridor, I heard my name being said in a room nearby.

That afternoon, when me and Axel were talking, a rather livid Josh came storming towards us. "You little swine!" He shouted, spit flying in all directions. "You! You! You liar!" His finger was pointing at me, his cheeks a hot red, like he was a kettle steam billowing out of his ears.
"Josh, I ...." I began.
"You are a traitor to me, Rebecca and The King and Queen!" He spat. "In fact, I am here to take you to them this very moment!" Josh, forcefully grabbing my arm dragged me out of the room as guards ran towards Axel, pulling him after us.
We entered the throne room. It was vast and golden, and an all-important throne sat at the back in the centre for all to see.
"Letty Lane and Axel Darlington, Your Highnesses!" He bawled.
The Queen stood to one side obviously not important enough to have a throne whilst a plump small man sat on his golden chair.
"So," he drooled, "so, I hear by my subjects you have committed treason?"
"No!" I shouted, "No! In the very least!"
"Guilty!" The King screamed. His double chin wobbling as he snapped his fingers at the guards. They stepped forward, advancing upon us. It was very clear to me that the King neither cared if we are guilty or innocent. The easiest thing for him to do to save himself any effort was to just sentence us to death.
"Your Highness! I implore you!" I screeched, but he simply sat there twiddling his thumbs and looking bored.
The guards yanked us away. I tried to fight them off but I felt

weak, like a young girl. I don't remember much, my mind seemed foggy as if someone had hit a blow to my head. I do remember sitting on a stone-cold floor though and feel people touching my hair from behind.

I had shrieked and moved away to realise men behind the bars I had been leaning on, had been stroking my hair. Some wolf whistled at me; others simply stared. "Letty!" Axel stood in front of me and pulled me to my feet, holding on to my elbows, so my weak knees might not send me to the ground.

"I don't understand!" I muttered, "What did we do?"

"It was probably just rumours, Letty. Lies to get rid of us, Josh and Rebecca must have found out we had snuck out last night and heard them."

"Rumours that have cost us our lives." I sat on the floor and thought for a long while. I remembered home and Grandpa Eddie and how he was completely bonkers. I remembered Mama and her roses and Papa and his fierce personality and love for horses. I remember Roy and his smell of oranges, his loving smile and charming laugh. I remember Roxanne and all those lives that have been lost. Little Harriet and how she had been so dear. Her sister and her grief.

So many people, so many lives thrown away and for a game of money and power. "Letty." Axel was saying to me. "Letty, I must tell you something." I gazed upwards through eyes full of tears. When he saw that, he smiled softly and wiped them with his finger.

Death was never something I had dreaded for myself but there I was, a girl standing with a boy holding her upright and fearing for her life. I had felt powerless, like already my life was ebbing away, I felt my death sentence was the end of my humanity. I had been stripped of the right of speech and it was just to save a fat old man on a throne from the trouble of a fair trial.

"Letty, we are to die, together at least. I am glad I shall perish to the King's punishment with you."

"Axel..." I breathed, taken aback by the sincerity of his words. "Love is always a pitiful thing, it makes you weak, prone to the fear of loss, I think we are different. I think we are stronger together than apart." The words fell from my mouth before I could stop them, and I felt the breath of Axel on my mouth.

The final goodbye

Smiling as wide as was wise, I laced my fingers with Axel's. His palm flush against mine. "Letty, Axel!" Came a wailing shriek and there, tears a blaze in her eyes, stood Bianca. She looked broken, torn to pieces. "Death? That is the Kings sentence? Death? How cruel can a man be!"

She wailed and buried her head in her hands. The men that had wolf whistled, grew very still and silent. Some sniffled as if they too were going to break into tears. "Oh Bianca." I clung to the bars, reaching my hands out to cup her cheek.

"I am so sorry!" I muttered.

Axel came to stand next to me and murmured, "You can live a better life now, one of a Lady. They were suspicious of us from the very start, I think! And Josh, I am sorry for his betrayal and for you sister as well!"

"Forget us B," I told her, "Live your life! If it pleases you, get married have children if not, do whatever your heart desires! We all only have one life don't spent yours in bereavement!"

She simply nodded her head, her blond locks falling in her eyes. Stepping away from us wearing an expression of deep pain and sorrow, she turned heal and without looking back walked up the stairs and left.

I turned back to Axel and muttered, "Poor soul. She must live a life of hatred towards those who swore to be her own blood and without the people who know her pain!"

Axel shook his head as if that movement could change dear Bianca's fate. I stepped forward once more and our hands clasped together like they were meant to fit next to each other, looking sadly into each other's eyes.

"Letty Lane." A cold voice came from behind me, and I turned to see the woman in black. "The creature Axel stabbed is wiser than me and my sister once thought. It has chosen to not return to us, we heard word that Nepheete saw it strolling along her waters far away from this kingdom and into a forest."

"I don't suppose you could help us cheat death this time Omisha?" Axel asked.

She smiled, her fangs glittering, "No. Death is as I told you once before, a game, when people cheat it, it ruins the fun."

"Indeed, sister," a sweet voice joined them as the woman in white advanced upon us. "I must admit I am sad to see you of all people so vulnerable to the cruelty of this world. Life did try to give you the best life you could live, but sometimes fate muddles with things."

Guinevere told us, "The only child of Lady Amelie shall grow up hearing stories about you two. I am sure Bianca shall help to tell her your tales." That made the corners of my mouth lift.

"Goodbye Axel. Letty." Then, walking back to the wall, both sisters vanished for the last time.

Later that evening, Josh sidled through the door, I ignored him as he called my name. "Letty! I meant not for you to die!"

"It matters not if this was what you were meant to do, for its happening and you cannot stop it. After all Josh, you are the moth."

"The moth?"

"Yes, the moth. You are attracted to the flame of greed and power. I wish not to speak to you ever again, be gone! And enjoy the life you clearly want!" I threw myself at the bars clinging to them knuckles turning white.

"Letty, you are a Lane, your whole family has died cowards and they shall be dishonoured in history! Mark my words!"

"Leave! Go!" He did so and just like Bianca did not look back.

That night I slept curled up next to Axel. Down there it was bitterly cold and there was no fire to warm us, or even a blanket or a sheet. There was no bed but the floor and little mountains of straw like we were animals.

I heard the men shuffling around us, settling down to sleep. The night gave me no sympathy, it made me stay awake, drowning in my sorrows and self-pity. Morning came with slow dread and when it came, I was suffering from deep misery. The clank of keys made me quake with fear and I had to be half carried out of the room.

Men cried prayers for God to have mercy on my soul and some spoke in languages even I did not understand. We were dragged, forced outside. I stared at my feet as I stumbled to my death place. I saw a block beneath me and looked up. Men and women surrounded me, The Queen, Bianca, Josh, and Rebecca in the front. The King it seemed had not been bothered to come.

Eternal sleep

It is not Letty who writes this chapter but I, Omisha. For Letty felt nothing but fear of death and she, like her lover, Axel, did not see anything but their own blackness.

Letty Lane took a breath in as she readied herself for her last words. They were beautiful, simple but perfect. "I die, Letty Lane, another disgrace to the Lanes name but would rather die Letty Darlington!"

Axels were just as memorable but less sweet, "When you foulmouthed people realise your mistake, I hope you live in guilt and despair."

Then two executioners stood on either side of them, waiting patiently. Together they kneeled, Letty Lane and Axel Darlington. They placed their heads on the block. Bianca covered her eyes and turned her back on the scene. A silence had crept over the crowd.

Death had stepped forward, not as enthusiastically as he normally did but with regret. He waited until the blow was struck and the screams of Bianca relinquished before sending the particles as bright as any floating into the sky.

It was a scene that people thousands of years later would retell to their children who would tell theirs and so on. The history of the Lane Twins and of Axel Darlington.

Rhea

A child, only 6, sat on her mother's lap, watching as the maids drifted by. Her mother was whispering words she could not quite understand. She had heard them before, but they were long and boring, and she knew not yet all the complicated things of the world she was only just starting to explore.

I know what those words were though, they were ones of sincerity and hope. Of the things the world seemed desperate of. She giggled contentedly as a butterfly flew by, donning the most charming orange and light blue. The mother saw what her child was looking at and whispered to her, "Harriet, my darling, would you like to hear a story? One of a girl? The flame of the story is called Letty Lane and the moths, the most dreadful beings…"

Author's Note

I hope you enjoyed this book! As a 12-year-old author, I would really appreciate it if you would leave a review on Amazon about my book even if just a few lines! It would really help me begin my future as an author and help other readers discover my books. I would be tremendously thankful and appreciative if you did, and it would really give me a boost — many thanks for reading this book.

Watch out for my next book, coming soon!